UNDER
TOWER
PEAK

Also by Bart Paul:

*Double-Edged Sword: The Many Lives of Hemingway's
Friend, the American Matador Sidney Franklin*

UNDER
TOWER
PEAK

by
Bart Paul

ARCADE PUBLISHING • NEW YORK

First Edition

This is a work of fiction. Names, characters, places, and incidents are either the products of the author's imagination or used fictitiously.

Arcade Publishing books may be purchased in bulk at special discounts for sales promotion, corporate gifts, fund-raising, or educational purposes. Special editions can also be created to specifications. For details, contact the Special Sales Department, Arcade Publishing, 307 West 36th Street, 11th Floor, New York, NY 10018 or arcade@skyhorsepublishing.com.

Arcade Publishing® is a registered trademark of Skyhorse Publishing, Inc.®, a Delaware corporation.

Visit our website at www.arcadepub.com.

10 9 8 7 6 5 4 3 2 1

Library of Congress Cataloging-in-Publication Data

Paul, Bart.
Under Tower Peak / by Bart Paul.—First edition.
    pages cm
ISBN 978-1-61145-836-7 (hardcover : alk. paper) —
ISBN 978-1-62872-434-9 (pbk : alk. paper) —
ISBN 978-1-61145-921-0 (ebook)
1. Veterans—Fiction. 2. Cowboys—Fiction. 3. Wilderness survival—Fiction.
4. Missing persons—Fiction. I. Title.
PS3616.A92765U53 2013
813'.6—dc23
                        2012043982

Printed in the United States of America

UNDER
TOWER
PEAK

When the cockpit got too warm, he crawled out of the plane and sat next to it. That was better. He rested with his back to the wreck beside the little pine and looked down the canyon across the tops of the snow-covered trees to the empty country from which he had come. At first he had been anxious, staring up at the big peak looming over everything, poking through the storm clouds, the northernmost point of this range. He turned to look at the wing sticking straight up through the snow and at the numbers painted on the wing, and didn't recognize them.

The last thing he remembered before feeling the jolt of the downdraft was glancing down at the map and seeing that the altitude of the peak was less than twelve thousand feet. Then he pushed the map away and got back to business, climbing to clear the pass—a shallow saddle coming up on him fast.

When he came to in the wrecked cockpit, he iced his head wound with snow until his hands were numb and then took an inventory, assessing his chances just as he always had. He thought of his wife and son and wondered when they were coming for him. There had been so much snow piled on the door he almost didn't have the strength to push it open.

Sitting outside was better now, but he was still warm. He snuggled down, feeling as if he were rushing through the air at two hundred miles an hour like the time his balloon hit a windshear in the jet stream as he soloed at twenty-seven thousand feet over the East China Sea. He was hot now and his head ached, and he remembered that his wife had died a long time ago, and that he must have another one somewhere. He laughed and took off his tee shirt. His son would never have the sense to find him up so high on the mountain to bring him home. He'd leave that to the pros. He looked back at the peak, but its spire was hidden now in the swirling white.

Chapter One

Early in the season we rode up to the forks to fix the trail above the snow cabin. The winter had been good and the aspens had leafed out down in the canyon at the edges of the meadows. Above The Roughs up in the tamarack pines it was shady and cool once the trail got narrow, and the only sounds were the steady scuff of the horses' hooves as they kicked up little puffs of dust and the clack when an iron shoe struck a rock as they climbed, the rush of the creek off in the timber, and the breeze through the tamarack limbs. The little mule just up-trail swung back and forth across our path on her leadrope, wasting her energy trying to get abreast of the front horse, and would have tired herself if she was packing anything in her slings heavier than shovels and saws.

We got to the snow cabin by midmorning and kept right on riding. It sat in the pines on a patch of boggy ground just below the forks, and was only in dappled sun even at midday. In a wet spring like this, the walls would be mossy and the place full of mosquitoes and spiders soon enough. We had spent the night there one January when we were in high school on one of our wild expeditions and were glad to have the shelter with the wind hammering over the pass, but our fire dried things out and made it livable inside. It wasn't built for summer anyway. The snow survey crews had stopped using the cabin years before. Now they choppered in, took their depth measurements and core samples and choppered back out. Some cross-country skiers had flown in back in the eighties when heli-skiing was the new hot ticket. They were going to glide down all the way from North Pass and spend the night in the cabin, then slog down over The Roughs into Aspen Canyon the next morning and hump it across the flat meadows all the way out to the valley, but it started snowing and they missed the cabin in the trees and froze to death. Their tracks showed two of them making crazy circles in the tamarack looking for it. One of those two was a pretty college girl, and she died just sixty feet from the cabin door. The body of a third was found far away down in the bare aspen below the meadows, heading in the right direction an easy few miles from the paved road. They never found the fourth body. That was all before our time, but it was that way more and more every year in the mountains—too easy to get in and too hard to get out. The door of the cabin hung lopsided on its hinges now, and city people had carved their initials on the logs.

At the forks we headed right, leaving the timber at the bottom of a rocky cirque, a big glacial bowl almost a mile across. Lester rode in front leading the little mule with the tools. She was one of Harvey's new mules and only half broke, so we wanted to put some miles on her before the season got rolling. We had the tools on her so if she pitched a fit she wouldn't damage our valuables. When she moved to run up on him, Lester would try to whap her across the nose with the end of her leadrope, but she got savvy and drew her head back every time. She was learning quicker than Lester. I rode behind, leading a big roan packhorse carrying our bedrolls and kitchen. He knew his business and I could barely tell he was there. We found the slide quick enough where an avalanche had left trees and rocks on the trail, just like the Forest Service had said. We picked a camp spot where there was a bit of grass below a seep then unpacked and hobbled the animals and went to work. Neither one of us wanted to spend more than a day and a night on this. We had too much to do back at the pack station, although it was nice to be up so high so early in the year with no flatlanders to babysit. The horses had put in a fair morning's work and would graze quiet in their hobbles for an hour or two before they got restless.

Lester didn't talk much, which wasn't how I remembered him, but he had wires in his ears and was listening to some music I couldn't hear. Come to think of it, that was always how it was with him, even before he got his tunes in his pocket. I could see him with that happy look of his, working to the music, at twenty-five still the crazy kid from before. Now and then he'd look over and grin like what we were doing was about the coolest thing in the world, which I guess to me now it was. I was up-trail, and for a long time there was nothing but that hard-work sound of a shovel blade slooshing into the sand or clanging on rock, or the back-and-forth of a bow saw or the thunk of an axe in a pine limb. Then behind me Lester fired up the chainsaw. I turned around at that. His shirt and hat were off and he was wearing Ray-Bans for safety goggles. Would've thought he was at the beach, although I'd bet it wasn't quite sixty degrees and we had to be getting close to nine thousand feet. There were patches of snow all around and a big snow-field filled the north-facing curve of the bowl all the way to where the trail tops out at North Pass. Lester would be one sunburned boy by dark.

"Guess we don't care about the law no more."

"What law would that be?" he asked.

"That no-machinery-in-the-Wilderness-Area law?"

"Who's going to know or care?"

"It's the law, is all."

"Who's going to turn me in Tommy, you?" He got that old crazy grin.

I went on shoveling. Lester laughed. Then about as nice as you please he sliced the bar of the saw through a jagged stub of avalanched pine that stuck out into the trail just high enough to take a rider's face off.

He eased off the throttle. "Okay, Mister Legal," he said. "We'd be up here another full day doing it your way."

The chain had covered his face with powdery sawdust. I never had very good arguments when Lester got a wild hair. He was right. We would've been up there a lot longer using just the axe and saw. As it was, we had that piece of trail squared away pretty quick.

It got cold fast once the sun went down. We watered the stock a last time after supper then tied them to a picket line and turned in early. I was watching the stars over Tower Peak and dozing off.

"You hear about the bears?" Lester asked.

"Nope."

"We had lots of bears come down last year," he said. "The winter before was so poor there was nothing growing and the bears were starving by June. Saw one over on Flatiron Ridge aggressive as hell. Walked into camp in broad daylight on his hind legs ready to kick ass and take names. He was so skinny he looked like a thin man in a cheap suit. Take away their meal ticket and they get nasty."

"Who don't?" I pulled the edges of my bedroll tarp around my head and set my hat over my face so I couldn't hear him as well.

"We had them coming down-canyon at night into the pack station all last summer raiding the trash." He'd seen me hunker down so he talked louder. "Me and Harv had to put a lock on the trailer to keep them from raiding the fridge."

"Go to sleep, Lester."

"A cute high school girl was backpacking up by Boundary Lake and woke up with a mama bear in her tent and her head in its mouth." He laughed. "Girl was wearing hair gel that smelled like grape jelly and that hungry old she-bear was licking it off her head like jam. Girl was lucky to live, but I bet she peed herself."

Next morning I was up before Lester, which was never much of an accomplishment. I'd slept like a baby myself. I led the stock two at a time from the picket line to the

North Fork of Aspen Creek about fifty yards off where it poured down through a tumble of rocks. It wasn't more than a couple of yards wide. When they'd had a good drink, I hobbled them apart on the patch of grass, each with a nice pile of grain in front of them. The cirque we camped in was steep and kept the first sunlight off us for a time, but the rim up near the pass and the snowfield got hit by those first rays while I was tending the stock. I always liked mornings the most in the high country. I'd spent too much time in the desert, so it was always good to get some altitude. I looked over across the bowl, and that snowfield was so bright I could have used Lester's shades. That's when I saw the plane. It was way across the bowl and up above us, just below the pass where the trail should be when the snow melted. A wing stuck straight up in the air, and it looked like the top of the plane was facing where I stood—like it was lying on its side. We had been working in plain sight of the wreck all the afternoon before, but it was a sandy-gray color and against the rocks and trees you could look right at it and miss it. Now the first sunlight hit the wing and the painted numbers and lit them up too. From as far away as I was, I couldn't tell how long that plane had been sitting up there, how big it was, or if there was any movement—if anybody was alive. I finished seeing to the stock, glancing up every now and again at the wreck. I pulled a rifle scope out of my saddle pockets and put the glass on that plane. It was a good scope and I'd got in the habit of carrying it. I could see a lot of detail and that just made the whole thing creepier. I didn't see any movement or any bodies, but there were some shapes and things I couldn't make out in the glare and shadows at way over a thousand yards.

Lester was still sleeping like a dead man when I built a fire and started breakfast. I couldn't even see him under his bedroll canvas, but it would be getting hot in there quick enough. Once the sun hit us and he smelled the coffee, he'd be up. If he didn't see the wreck for himself, as soon I told him about it he'd be like a kid and we'd have to ride right up there to see it, probably hiking the last quarter mile or so through the snow. Then god knows what the hell we'd find. We could be up there for hours. We still had some cleanup on the trail to do, then mules to shoe and corrals to fix and a generator to fiddle with once we got back. I was half a mind not to tell him at all.

He rousted out about fifteen minutes later, happy and chatty like always, and not at all bothered that the stock was already tended and breakfast was on the way. Truth be, if he had mentioned it I would have wondered just who the hell had kidnapped Lester.

"What Harvey needs to do," he said once I'd handed him his ham and eggs, "is send the Forest Service a bill."

"That so?"

"Sure," he said. "This is government property. A government trail. Government National Forest. A goddamn government avalanche no doubt caused by some fool bureaucrat sitting behind a desk. I think the old government should pay us for cleaning up this mess."

"I bet they'd pay right up just as soon as they knew it was Lester Wendover doing the work." I cut some more ham for the griddle.

9

"You're too forgiving, is your problem," he said.

I poured us both more coffee and glanced up at the plane. The longer I knew it was there, the more it stuck out. I couldn't move anywhere in camp and not see it, although it was pretty small with the naked eye. Lester sprinkled some Tabasco on his breakfast.

"Missed your damned scrambled eggs, old son," he said. "Most guys don't want to take the trouble and only pack the instant kind. They got no flavor."

"That's a fact."

"You ever break an egg?"

"Nope."

"Always pack 'em in the grain sack?"

"Duh."

"Along with the whisky, right?" he asked.

"I keep the whisky in my saddle pockets. A guy can live without eggs."

"Fifty years from now when they're hauling us up to the Piute Meadows cemetery, they'll be saying, 'That Tommy, he never did get rich, but damn he made good camp eggs.'"

We laughed, and I dragged a pail over from the creek and set it in the fire so Lester could wash the dishes.

We worked two hours dressing up the trail so you wouldn't hardly know there had ever been an avalanche, then we started to break camp and saddle up, sweating like stevedores although it was breezy and cool. The horses were restless and ready to travel. They knew that there was really no place to go but back on down the trail. I glanced up at the wreck. I guess somebody had to find it. And then there was the semi-remote chance that somebody might be alive in there. Hell. I waited till we both swung aboard.

"Say, Hawkeye, notice anything interesting?" We sat our ponies abreast, the pack animals behind us, our damp shirts cold in the breeze.

Lester turned. I didn't move. All that boy had to do was follow my eyes. He was pretty sharp. He saw that plane right off.

"Damn." He grinned and slapped me on the chest with the back of his hand. "Damn!"

He goosed his horse and off he went, that little mule skittering behind him to catch up after trying to buck once or twice, all of us clattering over the granite on the trail up to North Pass. For a time it was slow climbing, single file up through loose rock and thick mahogany. The stock was none too happy to be traveling hard away from home. The trail looped north around the cirque, away from the wreck at first. As we gained altitude it swung back around, kind of spiraling up the sides of the bowl. The animals picked their way and took their time. The higher we got, the bigger the patches of snow were on the trail, with wet spots of snowmelt in the rocks making them shine in the sun. We stopped to let the horses blow, and I pulled my scope out again to take a better look at the plane. I swept the reticle over the fuselage. It was like I was right on it. There was something ugly piled next to the plane. It still wasn't quite clear but I had a pretty good idea. Lester reached out and I handed him the scope. He squinted into it, then whistled.

"Damn," he said. He moved the scope up, checking the pass. "That plane is *all* messed up." He handed the scope back. "You know old son, I'm going to buy you some binoculars for Christmas."

"That'll be the day."

"How do you see through that?" he asked. "I can't hold it still enough."

"Just used to it, is all."

"It cost you a lot?" he asked.

"More than my dad paid for the rifle."

"Who made it?"

"Leupold."

"Leopold?" he asked.

"Leupold."

"Whatever. Count on old Tommy to have the best equipment."

I stowed the scope and we moved on. We finally hit a flat spot a hundred yards or more below the wreck at the edge of the steep snowfield that covered the switchbacks leading to the pass. I dismounted and we tied up to a couple of whitebark pines. Lester kept his eyes on the wreck. I listened hard, but the wind was the only sound.

"You think anybody's alive up there?" he asked.

"Soon find out. Best tie 'em tight. It's a long walk home."

"Let's go," he said.

"We should strip the packs. We might be up there a while."

Lester made a face but didn't argue. We spread the tarps on the ground and set the bags, boxes, bedrolls, ropes and slings on them. We loosened our cinches but left the animals saddled. Then we started to climb on foot.

The trail was buried from where we were all the way up to the wreck, so we made our own switchbacks in the bright snow. It was crusty, and in places an ice axe would have been handy, but mostly the footing was alright and we'd steady ourselves up by grabbing mahogany branches poking through the snow. Now and then we got off-trail and sunk through a melted spot or hit slick ice. When we stopped to catch our breath, we were under a steep slope and could only see the wing sticking up against the sky. Lester looked up at the ridges just above us beyond the pass, then back down from where we'd come.

"Boy," he said, "it's just us and god up here."

"Like he's watching."

"Well," he said, "what he don't know won't hurt him."

He nodded that he was ready and we set out again. He was getting excited. We were up close before we took another look up at the plane. Then Lester made a face.

The dark shape was a man, or what was left of one. We climbed the last few yards of the snowfield and stopped to catch our breath again about ten yards from the body. We looked around but didn't say anything for a while. Then we sidled up for a closer look. The man was naked and his skin was a blackish gray. He was sitting up against a rock like he was enjoying the view of the canyon. There were a few bits of clothes scattered around the open spot on the other side of the plane, and a pair of powder blue boxer shorts hanging from a stubby whitebark about six feet off the ground. The way the man was sitting with his back to the plane, we had to walk pretty close to get a look at his face. The eyes were gone and the lips peeled back, but the rest of him was pretty well preserved, more like a mummy than a corpse. Actually, he looked like something out of an old National Geographic, a photograph of a dead sailor from some Arctic expedition in the square-rigger days, or that Bronze Age guy who took an arrow up in the Alps. Bodies in ice. I could see a bit of chain around his neck with some sort of smudged-up medal attached. I looked close enough to see it was a medical alert, dog-tag style, with part of the word "diabetic" showing. I didn't feel like touching it to get a better look, and it was too late to matter anyhow. He had a big watch on that had slipped down to the top of his left hand, probably from his arm drying out. It looked like a pretty nice watch.

The plane looked like it had come up the canyon from the east and had crashed just a dozen feet lower than the pass. The nose rested on a granite outcrop right against the single whitebark pine where the boxers were hanging. Beyond the wreck was a good-sized open spot where new spring grass was just coming in with a few more trees on the downhill edge, but we were right at the timberline. Above us we could see the shallow saddle of North Pass only a hundred more yards up the trail that led over to Little Meadow on the other side. This was the crest of the Sierra, the dividing line. The nose of the plane was smashed a bit and the windshield cracked, but the way it nestled on those rocks up against that little tree, there was probably a lot more snow covering everything when it hit. The plane rested on its side like we noticed when we first saw it, and the right-hand wing was crumpled under it. The tail section stuck out just above ground and looked good to fly.

We both just stood there for a while, studying. Finally Lester made another face and picked up a stick and touched the body with it. It made a scratching sound like he was dragging it across cardboard.

"So," he said, "how come he ain't rotten? He didn't just light here."

"Nope. He's been here a while."

"How come the birds and critters didn't get him then?"

"You see any birds or critters?"

Lester shrugged. "Not many flies either," he said.

"We're up too high and it's too early in the year. He's probably been covered with snow most of the time. Give him another week with this melt and he'll get ripe enough, with critters to spare."

"But he's black around the edges," he said.

"Like freezer burn."

He nodded again and poked the body a second time with the stick. "He's just as hard and stiff as a fresh cowhide left out on a fence all winter."

"That's a fact."

He bent down to look at the watch, just shaking his head. "Damn," he said. Then he nodded at the boxers in the tree. "What's up with that?" he asked. "He trying to flag down help?"

"Hypothermia. Folks get out of their head and take off their clothes because they think they're hot."

"So if he didn't hang 'em in the tree," he said, "that must have been how deep the snow was when he shucked 'em."

"You're probably right."

15

We heard a sound then, a rumbly drone like a helicopter. We both looked over the mountains but couldn't see a thing. There were fifty mile views off east, but peaks and ridges up close hid it.

"Maybe that's County," Lester said. "Maybe somebody already called this in."

I listened another minute. We could hear the chopper get closer and louder. For a minute it fairly shook the mountain but we still couldn't see it.

"That's a Sikorsky. Probably from the Marine base."

Lester left the body and walked around the wreck.

"You think there's another body inside?" he asked.

The helicopter got faint until we couldn't hardly hear it, probably heading back north toward the training camp off Sonora Pass.

"I doubt it. But hey, go look. I've seen enough bodies."

"You're not curious?" he asked.

"Not a bit."

Lester didn't hunt for more bodies right then. He just looked at me. He was getting a kind of smile. He took his hat off and looked at it then put it back on.

"So how long," he said, "do you figure this guy lived after the crash?"

"Too long to be happy about it, that's for sure."

"Seriously," he said.

"Anywhere from about ten hours to a couple of days. No more, though. Wasn't dressed for it."

Lester pondered some more. You could almost see him getting excited like he'd just figured something out.

"How long you figure this guy's been up here?" he asked.

"Months."

"Not weeks?"

"Nope."

"Not years."

"No."

Then Lester got one of his big grins and started shaking his head.

"Are you thinking what I'm thinking, Tommy?"

"Could be."

"It's him," he said. "That millionaire."

"Billionaire's more like it."

"Yeah. The eccentric billionaire adventurer. The round-the-world balloon racer and land-speed record guy. That daredevil, airplane-flying sonofabitch. How long ago did he just up and disappear?" he asked.

"Early last winter. Been months and months."

Lester's eyes got real bright. "It's him, alright. It all fits. It's *him*." He walked up close to the corpse. "Man, did you get a load of this watch?"

He looked hurt when I laughed, which was hard enough to do with that mummy sitting there without his boxers.

"Well if it's him, his daredevil days are history."

Lester just spit. "He takes off from the Flying W last winter for a little cruise around the hills," he said, "then poof. He vanishes, right?"

"You're telling it."

"Disappears off the face of the earth. Guys at that airplane club said he filed no flight plan, just wore a windbreaker over a tee shirt, and didn't pack so much as a damn sandwich," he said. "Some big adventurer."

"He probably didn't figure on smacking into the mountain."

"They never figured on the mountain," he said, trying to sound like a movie trailer.

I started walking around the wreck myself, taking a better look this time. Lester followed me, just full of the devil. Inside I saw blood splattered on the instruments and a pilot's map, plus a blue windbreaker. All told, there was less damage than I would have figured.

"That private airstrip on the Flying W is what," Lester said, "about forty, maybe forty-five miles northeast as the crow flies?"

I stopped and let him catch up.

"Why, I used to buckaroo for the Flying W when we were in high school," he said.

"You were only the chore boy for the Flying W cowboss at Longmile and you know it."

"Well, I know that Nevada country," he said, "and so do you. That old boy could fly this thing from there, over the state line to here in a half hour I bet, give or take."

Lester studied the plane again, poking the skin. He unfolded his knife and sliced the fuselage. It was fabric and cut like a pup tent.

"Jesus," he said. "This sucker is as small and flimsy as a ride at the tri-county fair."

"That would be the point, wouldn't it? Make them light so they fly and not sink?"

"But this is just tubes, rags, and an engine," he said. "I bet it's old as hell. I thought this guy was loaded."

"It was a borrowed plane, bud."

He got a happy look. "There's got to be a reward, right?"

"Probably so."

"Old son," he said, "we just struck ourselves rich."

"Don't spend it till you get it."

"Ahh," he said. He waved me away like he used to. He stood there with his hands on his hips, looking around as contented as could be. Then he looked up past North Pass and pointed.

"That's Hawksbeak, right?"

"Hawksbeak's this one on the left. That one's Tower."

Lester took off his hat and wiped his face, still just amazed as hell.

"Would you look at that," he said. "Another fifteen feet higher, and this old fellow is home free. He cruises over the pass and—whoosh. If he had enough gas, he could keep the same altitude and there'd be nothing else in his way all across California. He could fly all the way to China before he hit anything. Damn. Just fifteen lousy feet." He kinda shrugged. "Oh well. His loss is our gain." He kicked the fuselage. "Maybe he was bopping around for hours taking in the views and flat ran out of gas."

"You're probably right."

"You just always remember you said that."

"I'm going back down and grab some food and make sure we're not afoot. You about done here?"

"No sir," he said. "I want to check his gas tanks." With the wreck on its side, the cabin door opened upwards like a trapdoor. He started to pry it open.

"Lester?"

He turned around.

"Don't go messing with anything. This man died here, so show some respect. Besides, if he is who we think he is, the Feds and his family and cable news will be all over this, not just the county sheriff. It wouldn't do to have stuff tampered with."

"Sure Tommy," he said. "But this is still the chance of a lifetime." He grinned. "We'd kick ourselves till our dying day if we didn't at least check it out. Come on. Don't be a wussy. Let's just take a little peek-a-roon."

"You take a peek. I'm hungry. And like I said, I seen enough bodies."

I walked around the plane to the edge of the snowfield and headed back down following the tracks we'd made, trying not to slip on my ass. The animals down below were standing quiet for now. I snugged down their leadropes then rooted in the kitchen box for sandwich fixings and apples and a water jug. I looked up across the snowfield but couldn't see Lester from where I stood. I ate my apple and divided a couple more among the stock. I called for Lester, but he didn't answer. Then I hiked back up.

Lester was just crawling out of the wreck when I got to the top and caught my breath.

"There's a tank under each wing," he said. "They aren't any bigger than the one on that old Volkswagen Bug Doreen Rountree had in the tenth grade."

"Still probably enough to give him a couple hundred cruising miles."

"I thumped them and they sounded empty." He held up a piece of wire. "I'm gonna check for sure." He stepped under the wing and unscrewed the gas cap and stuck in the wire. He held it up for me.

"Just a teeny bit wet on the tip," he said. "This boy flat ran out of gas and that's a fact."

"Could be at this altitude it just evaporated. It's been months."

He looked disappointed. "Yeah, maybe," he said. Then he got that excited look again.

"So, what do we do about all this?" he asked.

"What do we do? What do you mean what do we do, Lester? We report it, is what."

"Okay," he said, "but what if there's a reward?"

"We'll make the report to the sheriff's office on our way to Harvey's tonight. Then if there's some reward, folks will know it's us."

"I don't know," he said. "We might want to contact the guy's family first. They shouldn't be hard to find. Then they could call the sheriff, or ask us to." He gave me a happy look. "We'd tell them we'll do whatever they say. They'd owe us, then."

"How about we just tell the sheriff's office like we would if we'd found any other body."

"But Tommy," he said, "this isn't any other body."

"That's why we tell the sheriff. Jesus Lester, give it a rest."

"Okay," he said. "Tell you what, Tommy. Let's swear that this is our secret and nobody else's."

21

"Why? We back in the third grade all of a sudden?"

"So it's just our secret," he said.

"Won't mean much once we tell the sheriff."

"Just swear," he said.

"Okay, I swear."

That made him happy enough. We found a spot beyond the wreck on that little flat bit of grass and ate our sandwiches sitting on some rocks.

"This kinda gives me the creeps," he said.

"Yeah."

But he didn't look like he had the creeps. Lester actually looked pretty pleased with the whole deal.

"It sure is a lonesome place to die," he said.

"Any place is a lonesome place to die."

Within half an hour we were packed up and riding back down to the forks.

Chapter Two

We got back to the pack station around five that afternoon with loads of daylight left. We turned our stock loose in the pasture with the few head of saddle horses we'd left behind, tossed some hay in the mangers, and flipped for the first shower. In another half hour we were on the road down the mountain in Lester's new Ford Dually with a couple of sixpacks for company.

We turned off the logging road and cruised out through the irrigated meadows with the sundown behind us, Bonner and Tyree's cattle on the right side of the road and Dominion's on the left. I was out of practice on the saw and shovel work we'd been doing, so I felt a little sore-muscled, but it was a good kind of sore. Lester was smiling to himself.

"So what do you think old Mitch will say about us finding this plane?" he asked.

"You know him. He's the damn sheriff. He'll grouse and say he wished it had crashed over the pass in Alpine County out of his jurisdiction."

"But if that old boy had made it over the pass," Lester said, "he never would have crashed."

"That won't stop him from saying it."

"So how long you figure Mitch'll keep us?" he asked.

"Half hour, maybe. They got good maps. We can show them right where it is."

"Then we should be up at Harvey's for supper about, let's see now," he stretched his arm out and looked down at a big shiny gold watch, "about seven-thirty." He turned and grinned while he was still going sixty-five.

"Jesus Christ, Lester. You stole the damn watch."

He looked kind of hurt. "He wasn't using it."

"You took a watch off a dead man."

"It's not just a watch," he said. "It's a chronometer."

"Are you nuts?"

"It's a twenty-grand gold Rolex, Tommy, give or take."

"Buy your own damn watch. Jesus, Lester."

He reached into his jacket pocket and took out a thick wad of cash and stuck it in my face. Looked to be mostly hundreds.

"Okay," he said. "I will."

"Christ. Stop the truck."

"There's enough there for you to buy one too."

"Stop the goddamn truck."

He shut the Ford down right on the road. Wasn't anyplace to pull over. From the pavement it just sloped down to the barbwire fence. He looked like he was thinking real hard. The diesel idled away as a tourist camper blasted by us in the opposite direction heading toward Summers Lake. He flashed his lights at us though it wouldn't be sundown for a while yet.

"Tommy," he said, "this guy is worth hundreds of millions. His damn lawyers are going to steal more from his damn estate in the next twenty-four hours than I got in my pocket." He banged on the steering wheel. "He had almost eighteen thousand cash on him. Four thousand in his wallet, the rest in a paper sack." He grinned then. "Along with a turkey sandwich, which looked about as sorry-assed as he did." He shrugged. "I took about eight K from the sack and nothing from the wallet. That's all, Tommy. Eight lousy grand. Enough to pay off the truck or marry Callie Dean."

"Listen to yourself."

He got kind of mad then. He jerked a Coors from the sack and popped it open. He guzzled down a mouthful and put the Ford in gear and floored it.

"Don't go getting high and mighty on me, Tom."

We didn't say anything the next four miles into Piute Meadows. He knew I was steamed. He threw his empty can behind the seat and turned a sharp right on to the main street, then a left at the courthouse. A block behind that he hit the brakes hard in front of the sheriff's office.

"Well?" he said. "Now what?" The boy wouldn't even look at me.

"You know damn well what. We can't go in there with you wearing the dead guy's watch."

He got an I-got-you look and moved the truck out again, driving slow this time. At the corner he turned away from Main Street and started to circle the block.

"Tell me why," he said.

"You know damn well. Once we report it tonight, they'll have him helo-ed out by tomorrow noon. His family will get notified and come on up here. Then they'll have to ID the body and the belongings. Then pretty soon somebody from the family or one of his rich Flying W airplane pals will wonder where did that gold Rolex get to? And what happened to that eight thousand? And since you and me were the only ones up there, old Tommy and Lester will be branded all over CNN and Nancy Grace and the whole damn world as a couple of shitsucking body robbers."

"Come on."

"I ain't no body robber and I won't be known as one."

"Okay," he said, "easy now."

He had circled the block, and we were cruising slow past the front of the sheriff's office again. There were a couple of white Ford Expedition cruisers out front with the Frémont County badge on the door.

"Let's think about this," he said.

"Nothing to think about, Lester."

"We could say that the whole deal had been messed with before we got there." He said that like it was a good idea.

"I won't start lying so don't ask me to."

"Or maybe one of those hungry bears chewed that watch clean off." He laughed at himself. We turned left for a second trip around the block. The cinderblock office and jail was about the only thing on the block, so we'd be getting company pretty quick if he kept circling.

"Listen to yourself, Lester. Tell one lie and you got to tell another to explain it."

"You said yourself we can't report this now," he said, "right?"

"Round one for you, assbite. But get ready to saddle up, because we are riding back to that wreck in the next forty-eight hours and you are putting that watch and that money back where you found it."

"Sure, Tommy," he said, "sure. You worry too much. Say, I wonder what May's cooking for dinner tonight?" He grinned like he always did. "Why I'm so hungry I could eat a bear myself."

He stuck his headphones in his ears, fiddled with the volume on his little music player, and off we went. We turned off the Reno Highway five miles south of town onto the dirt road that climbed through the sagebrush up to Power Line Creek. Fifteen minutes later Lester parked next to Harvey's stock truck tucked in the pines and boulders by the corrals. It was still light out, but there were electric lights on in the cabin and the sound of a TV. We went inside.

"Greetings, Lindermans," Lester said. He was carrying the paper sack.

Harvey looked up from his *San Francisco Chronicle*, fiddling with his fork and looking sour. May looked over from the stove.

"Hey handsome," she said to Lester, "hey Tommy." She handed a bowl of baked beans to her grandson parked in front of cartoons and pointed the little kid to the table.

I took off my hat and set it on a chair, and we both went over and gave May a kiss on the cheek like always.

"You get that trail done?" Harvey asked like we hadn't.

Lester and I glanced at each other for a quick second.

"Sure did," Lester said. He smiled like he didn't have a worry in the world. "Tommy was a little rusty though. Forgot how to use a chain saw. Right, Tom?"

"Forgot, huh?" Harvey said.

"There's one spot we got to do yet. Below the place the Forest Service sent us. Lester and I'll ride back in a day or so."

Harvey just grunted at me.

"Shouldn't take us more than a couple of hours."

"It can wait," Harvey said. "We got horses and mules to shoe before that Boy Scout trip to Hornberg Lake on the twenty-eighth."

"You think the snow will be clear by then?"

"It better," Harvey said, "or I lose a bundle. I wonder if leasing this damn second pack station was such a goddamn good idea."

"Where's Albert?" Lester asked. "He's the mule-shoeing genius here."

"Sheriff's got him in the drunk tank again," Harvey said. "I was supposed to pick him up this afternoon but never got to it."

"Well, shoot, Harv," he said. "Me and Tommy was just practically at the sheriff's. We could've picked him up for you if we'd known."

"I can never get you on that goddamn new phone you carry," Harvey said.

"Nobody can," Lester said. "That's the beauty of it. Drives Callie crazy." Lester took his phone and set the wires in the little boy's ears then fiddled with the screen and handed the whole outfit to him. The kid started bobbing his head to the tunes.

"Now I'll have to buy him one of his own," May said, but we could see she was tickled. She turned off the TV.

"Those goddamn phones are just going to get better," Harvey said. "Backpacker does something stupid in the high country, gets himself hurt or stranded, he just calls the Forest Service with his GPS location and they hire a damn helicopter to haul 'em out and we pay for it."

We'd all heard this tear before and knew best not to interrupt. I reached over and yanked Lester's hat off his head and tossed it on the couch. May was too old fashioned to like men wearing hats in the house but too old fashioned to complain.

"Jay-sus Chroist," Harvey said, "one of these days the Forest Service will let them damn 'copters haul campers in during the summer like they haul skiers in during the winter and us packers will be damn dinosaurs."

It got real quiet for a minute. Then Lester pulled a six-pack of Coors out of the sack and set it on the table.

"Hell, Harv," he said. "Everybody knows you're a dinosaur already. That's what May says."

May laughed and Harvey's eyes got some devilment in them then and he took a Coors. We grabbed a couple ourselves and sat down. The little boy turned at the three tops popping. Lester pulled a Hansen's soda from the sack and held it up.

"School out, Darryl?" he asked the boy.

Darryl pulled a wire out of one ear. "Yessir."

"What grade you in next year?"

"Fourth." The boy took the soda.

"What do you say?" May said.

"Thanks," Darryl said.

May set a platter of ribs on the table and we dug in.

"Always the charmer, Les," she said.

The boy put the wire back in his ear, and we quit talking for a bit and got serious about gnawing on those bones. After a while I could see Lester make of show of thinking about something like it had just occurred to him.

"Say Harv," he said. "You think they'll ever find that missing billionaire that disappeared off the Flying W?"

"I doubt it," Harvey said. "If they haven't found him by now there probably ain't much to find." He reached for another Coors. He was already in a better mood.

"When that old boy first flew off the map, that was all folks around here talked about," Lester said. "Now you don't hear much on it. Just barroom talk, like whatever happened to Frémont's cannon."

"People said he disappeared on purpose," May said, "but I don't believe it. Why would he leave all his money?"

"Maybe his wife was a terror," Harvey said, winking at Darryl.

May flicked her napkin at him, but he jerked his head back like the mule Lester had been leading.

"Come on, Harv," Lester said, "I bet you could find him if anybody could. You used to mustang out in that Flying W country when you were a young one."

"Too much country is why," Harvey said. "Too many places to disappear."

"That is," Lester said, "if that's where he crashed. What if he came as far west as here?"

"There's wrecks up in these mountains that nobody's found," Harvey said. "Dozens. Back to World War Two. There's a lot of country back up here. Jay-sus, I ought to know. If somebody does spot that bastard, it'll be some goddamn backpacker and he'll get that reward."

"There is no reward," May said, "at least not from the family."

"No reward?" Lester said. "That's crazy, May."

"That's what I read anyhow," she said. "I just think that's shameful." She turned to Lester and me. "If Harvey disappeared, I'd at least offer up the truck."

We all laughed at that, even Darryl.

"Actually," May said, "that guy has another billionaire friend from England who's put up ten thousand, but not one penny from the wife or son."

"I heard the son paid for some of the searching," Lester said. "Hired planes, led flyovers, and all that. Funny about the wife, though."

"Maybe he pissed his wife off," Harvey said, "farted in bed."

"There'd be a whole lot more missing husbands if that was the case," May said.

"You think me and Tommy could find that wreck?" Lester asked.

"Now I don't know," Harvey said, "Maybe. Tommy here was always a damn fine hunter."

31

"Come on, Harv," he said, "are you saying I couldn't find that plane?"

"You gotta be smarter than a watermelon to eat one, Les," Harvey said, "so the jury's still out." Harvey had no teeth on top so when he laughed he looked downright mischievous.

"Maybe he flew over Area Fifty-One and saw some space aliens," Lester said.

"Here he goes," Harvey said to May.

"Seriously Harv," Lester said, "maybe Mister Billionaire saw something he wasn't supposed to see and the government shot him down. They could be holding him on Moonbase Five right now. Isn't that so, Tommy?"

"Only space case I know oughta pass me that coleslaw before I beam his ass up."

May gave me a funny look. "You're being awfully grumpy tonight, Tommy."

"That guy's plane went off the radar before I got back to this country. I got nothing to say about it."

Lester fiddled with his beer can, then finished it off and picked up Harvey's paper.

"So," he said, "how are your Giants doing this year?"

"Off to a goddamn lousy start," Harvey said, "like that's a big surprise. Where's that goddamn Barry Bonds when a guy needs him?" He pushed himself away from the table and scratched his belly. "If Albert stays drunk, I'll need you boys to do some shoeing up here, too."

We both nodded.

"Seems like Albert Coffey's been drunk as long as I can remember," Lester said. "Drunk and horny."

"Longer," May said. "He hasn't been the same since Vietnam. He's had a hard time."

"I don't know," Lester said. "You'd think after almost forty years a guy would get over it, wouldn't you, Tom?"

I reached for another beer, but Harvey had drunk the last one.

"Nosir, I sure wouldn't think that at all."

We had some ice cream, then got in the truck and headed off down the mountain.

Chapter Three

"May's right," Lester said. "You are in one piss-poor mood, old son."

We were rattling downhill through the sagebrush on the washboard road in the early dark, heading back toward the Reno Highway. It was about a quarter past nine.

"For a guy who wanted us to swear never to tell nobody about the wreck, you sure as hell were dropping hints."

"I just wanted to find out what Harvey knew," he said.

"You were about to spill it, bud."

"Oh they didn't catch on."

"I known Harvey and May my whole life. They're what makes this valley. Them and the old ranchers. Now I'm lying to 'em."

He just shrugged it off.

"Let's go out to the lake," he said. "See Callie Dean."

I pulled a bottle of Crown Royal from under my jacket. "You're the one driving."

I took a drink and handed him the bottle. He grinned and took it like we were eighteen and off to Reno on a Saturday night. I'd figured that after a couple days away from that girl, he wouldn't be wanting to take the time to drop me off at the pack station before he took a run at her, so I'd come prepared.

On the main street of Piute Meadows there were new pickups and campers and trailers parked in front of the bars and motels, tourists on their way to the campgrounds and trailheads. When we'd crossed the meadows, instead of turning up the logging road, we kept on the blacktop toward Summers Lake. Truth be, I didn't mind. You forget just how it is, a deep pocket set under the high peaks, timber on the ridges and the breeze ruffling the aspen and pines along the shore, and the light of the stars or moon or even headlights on the deep water.

Callie was house-sitting a vacation cabin. The owners were city people who only came up a week or two all summer. When they came, she would go back to her crummy apartment behind the general store. The paved road followed the water's edge. It dead-ended at the ramshackley campground and boat rental at the far end of the lake at the Yosemite trailhead half a mile beyond the cabin. Lester turned off on a dirt drive marked by the owners' name carved on a wooden sign. The cabin sat a hundred feet above the lake buried in thick aspen. You could hardly see it when you drove by.

Callie was up watching *Bones* on TV when we piled in. We got some glasses and ice and put a dent in the

Crown Royal before she dragged Lester off to bed. The cabin was sixty years old and had a big main room like a lodge with two stairways running up each side and a stone fireplace with a buffalo head hanging over it. That there'd never been buffalo in our part of the West didn't bother these folks. A buck would've made more sense. In the aspen uphill from the cabin the mule deer were as common as flies. Any fall you could fill your tag from the kitchen window.

"You mountain men don't look any the worse for wear," Callie said. She got up for more ice. "How was it up in the great beyond?" She flounced into the kitchen in a shorty robe. Lester couldn't take his eyes off her.

"Nothing special."

"Don't listen to him," Lester said. She came back in and freshened our drinks. "The trails were open and we were high enough to see all the way out to the Flying W range."

He got up and grinned at me like he just couldn't help himself. He was following Callie up one of the staircases.

"There's clean sheets in the master bedroom, Tommy," Callie said. "See you in the AM."

"I'll just flop on the couch. Besides, I want to run down something on the web. These tofu-munching gunsels have Wi-Fi?"

Callie pointed down to a laptop glowing on a couch. "They got everything, hon," she said. She nodded across to the opposite staircase. "Really, use the bedroom. They wouldn't mind."

"Wouldn't want to get comfortable in a house that wasn't mine."

"God, Tommy," she said, "you are such a hard case."

"That's what she says about me," Lester said, dragging her into the bedroom and shutting the door.

I topped off my drink and fired up the laptop. It didn't take me long to find all sorts of sites on the missing billionaire. There was blog nonsense about where he might have crashed, did he crash at all, or was he hiding out somewhere, and what kind of plane he was flying. Some of them sounded like Lester, saying the government either killed him or was holding him in some desert Guantanamo in the middle of Nevada because he saw what was supposed to stay hid. They said the wreck was stashed in some guarded hanger at some secret base out east of Tonopah—that sort of craziness. I learned that his wife lived in a high-end part of Los Angeles, and that she wasn't his first. Some folks trashed her like May Linderman had for not putting up a reward. They said she had more money than god, or would have soon enough. I read stuff about a son about thirty-five years old from the first wife who had died some time back. The son seemed like a no-account. He owned a helicopter business in Miami Beach that the dad had staked him to. He'd had scrapes with the law and hung out with bad companions. But when his dad's flying pals didn't keep him in the loop during the search, he'd hired local pilots to look for his old man. Maybe he wasn't such a useless tool after all. You can find just about anything on a computer if you stay up all night.

When the noise up in the bedroom got aggravating, I took my drink out to the deck. It was ringed by aspen and Jeffrey pine so thick you could barely see the paved road down below. This late at night there were no cars, only that huge ridge rising straight up off across the lake and that dark water just as still as you please. Above it all were granite peaks. I could see the one they called the Cleaver. It seemed far away and lonesome and cold. It was hard to believe Lester and I had climbed it when we were seventeen. We'd ridden up the night before our day off, camped at a lake with good grass at almost ten thousand feet, then hiked up at dawn and climbed that sucker from the back side then rode our horses home down narrow switchbacks in the dark. That was a day. I couldn't figure owning such a place as this cabin and not spending every day in it, even if there wasn't a place to keep a horse.

I went back in and picked up the computer again. There wasn't any picture of the dead guy's wife, but I found a video on YouTube of the son from a Florida air show a year before. He was doing a power-off landing in a helicopter from a couple hundred feet, letting the rotors slow the fall. I'd heard about army pilots trying that, but on the tape it looked dicey as hell, too easy to get off balance, flip over and fall like a rock, then crash and burn. I rode bad horses from time to time and didn't think too much of it, but I never felt safe in a helicopter. The son either had big *cojones* or was flat out of his mind. Or both. At the end of the video this idiot-stick walked up to the camera with some blond. He was wearing shades and a muscle shirt and some gay-looking fake cowboy hat like you see skiers or actresses wear, so I couldn't see his face. He shouted something at the camera and did pointy, gang-sign non-sense with his fingers. If his old man had ever seen that video, the crash up by North Pass was pure suicide.

"Hey you," Callie said, "don't you ever sleep?"

It was only about midnight, and she was skipping down the stairs to pee. She stood over the couch in her nightie watching me.

"Don't want to fall asleep. They catch you when you do."

"Who catches you, hon?"

"The bad guys, darlin'. The bad guys never sleep."

Callie smiled. "This is heaven on earth, remember? There are no bad guys here."

She sounded so damn sincere I thought she'd break my heart.

"You just keep thinking that, gorgeous."

She scurried off to the bathroom. When she came back her hair was brushed and she looked as fine as always. She plopped herself next to me and kissed me on the cheek.

"Do I smell good?" she asked.

"You know what you smell like."

"My god, Tommy, you are such a prude. You should have been a preacher." She twirled a finger in the hair over my ear. "Have you been surfing the web since bedtime?"

"I spent some time on the deck just watching things."

"It is beautiful," she said. "The woman that owns this place says it reminds her of Switzerland."

"Bullshit. Switzerland reminds itself of us."

"So, cowboy," she said, "tell me all about that airplane."

I looked at her, but I didn't say a word. Goddamn Lester.

About then he opened the bedroom door and came out on the landing just wearing a towel. He looked thrashed.

"Howdy, buckaroos and buckarettes," he said. "Hell, old son, you still up?"

"So you kept our secret for what—two hours?"

"I was tortured," he said. "She has ways."

"So I heard."

Callie giggled at that.

"Swearing a secret was your idea, bud."

Lester just shrugged as he sauntered down the steps.

"Isn't he just the cutest," Callie said. "With that towel and surfer-boy blond hair, he looks like he should be on some beach in Hawaii."

Lester was just eating it up.

"I should buy you a puka-shell necklace, babe," she said. "Wouldn't he look precious, Tommy?"

"He'd look guaranteed to get himself stomped in Elko is what he'd look like. Jesus Christ, Lester, put some pants on."

He laughed and went off to the bathroom.

Callie gave me a funny look. "He hates the name Lester," she said. "Everybody calls him Les except you."

"Lester is his name. It's about all his daddy ever gave him but grief, and what Missus Huntoon called him in the sixth grade."

"So?"

"So I call him Lester just to aggravate him."

"You can be such a dick, Tommy Smith."

"Calling him that keeps him humble. Be no living with him otherwise."

"He worships you, you know," she said. "He thinks you hung the moon."

"I don't know what to think about talk like that." I had to look at her then. "I do surely wish he had a pinch of caution."

She gave me a sweet kind of look. "If he had," she said, "he wouldn't be our Les and we wouldn't love him so."

"If he had, he wouldn't try so hard to get his dingus in a wringer about this dead guy."

"Les says he wants to contact the man's family," she said, "but you don't."

"I just want to report the wreck to the sheriff and stay the hell out of it."

"You're no fun."

"Calling the sheriff is sort of like the chain of command. Then old Mitch can contact who-the-hell-ever he thinks is best. You get off that chain, things get complicated mighty quick and folks start asking questions you can't answer."

"You think too much." She kissed my cheek again.

"Cut that out." I turned the laptop to where she could read it.

Callie cuddled up smelling musky and good, her face lit up by the screen. She pulled the Mexican blanket covering the couch over her legs to keep warm. Pretty soon she was clicking and scratching away.

I was finally dozing off when she elbowed me.

"Boy," she said, "the wife and the son are definitely not on the same page. If our billionaire was trying to disappear, they're the reason why."

"He ain't our billionaire."

"Go back to sleep," she said, but she kept on talking. Then I noticed Lester sitting in the couch opposite, watching us.

"The wife has been to court in L.A. to get the guy declared legally dead, but the son in Miami says the old guy's taken a powder before and will turn up sooner or later," she said. "I say we call them both then just stand back." She pushed the computer away and fairly bounced off the couch. She landed on the other one next to Lester without enough nightie to do the job.

"Nothing like a billion dollars to get folks fighting among themselves," she said. "We could get rich on the spillage."

"You're crazy, woman."

"Knowledge is power," she said, "and right now nobody knows about that wreck but us."

"And in about thirty hours once that watch and the cash . . ."

"And the cash?" Lester asked.

"Yeah, the cash too. Once it's back with the body, the sheriff will get told. Then if there's some sort of reward, like from that English guy, then Lester can have some money and you can sleep with a clear conscience."

"I'd rather sleep with a billion dollars," Callie said, mussing Lester's hair, "or the hot guy who's got it."

I stretched out on the couch and closed my eyes. These two were wearing me out.

I rousted Lester before sunup. He wasn't any easier to wake up after a night in the sack with Callie than he was after a night in camp fixing trail, but he wasn't any harder either. I was itching to grab a microwave breakfast from the store at the campgrounds then blast on up to the pack station and shoe a couple of horses while we still had the gumption, but while Lester was in the can Callie skipped down the stairs in that nightie, gave me a big smile, and threw open the refrigerator. Every time I think that girl is eight kinds of useless and trampy, she pulls a stunt like that—breakfast steak, Mexican omelet, toast, coffee, and melon. While she was cooking I used the house landline to phone my mom in Jack's Valley near Carson City where she did bookkeeping for a polled Hereford outfit. The first sun was just hitting the ridges above the lake when we piled into the truck for Aspen Canyon.

We were clinching the nails on the last hind foot of the second mule when we heard Harvey's GMC coming off the hill through the trees. The truck disappeared, but we heard the rattle of the stock racks then the whinny of the horses as he drove over the bridge. We unloaded the six head at the chute, then got Harvey some coffee from the trailer. It was about ten in the morning.

"You get these 'morphadites shod, I guess you can finish that trail section tomorrow if you think you ought to," he said. "I don't want the goddamn Forest Service asking why the next time they ride through there and find it ain't done."

"Now, it's not so bad," Lester said, "that it couldn't wait a few days. Maybe we should stay here and tighten up the loading chute."

"Let's get it done, Lester. The season starts we'll never get the time." I buckled my chinks back on over my jeans and grabbed a halter to catch one of the new horses I remembered from years past. They hadn't had shoes since Lester and Albert had jerked them in November before they were trucked down to Nevada for the winter. "We'll ride up there tomorrow, Harv."

Harvey grunted and walked over to the generator. It was a big Navy-surplus Caterpillar diesel that wasn't worth the trouble to keep running. It sat on its own trailer and was so damn noisy and smelly I never liked using it in the summer. We could get by with kerosene lamps and the propane stove and fridge until deer season when we needed it for yard lights. Lester had replaced the glow plugs and some battery cables the week before.

"You got this running?" Harvey asked.

Lester shrugged, looking pleased with himself. "Fire it up," he said.

Harvey walked around to the back, flipped a big switch, then pushed the starter and fired it up. Black smoke chugged out. He looked pretty surprised.

"Not bad for boys," Harvey said. He had to shout over the noise, but he was smiling. The thing had a muffler running along the top as big as a water heater. After about a minute it sputtered and died and we couldn't get it started again.

"Jay-sus Chroist," he said, "check the fuel filter and the damn alternator. I got a Delco-Remy down at my shop in Hudson might work on the sonofabitch. Damn."

In another half hour, after we'd talked about the generator some more, talked about which horses we'd keep here on pasture until the Boy Scouts came to Power Line Creek in ten days, talked about the Forest Service which would be damn grateful for all the trail work he was doing for them, and talked about the Giants' improved bullpen, he climbed into the GMC and drove off. We watched the truck disappear in the aspens then rattle over the bridge and climb the hill before either of us opened our mouths.

"Don't you backtrack on me, Lester."

"I wasn't backtracking," he said. "I just thought riding up there could wait a day."

"It can't wait. As long as we know, it can't wait at all. What if someone else sees that wreck from the air, reports it, then you'd get called a goddamn body robber the rest of your life."

"What someone else would be flying around up there?" he asked.

"There is always someone else."

I tied up an old horse to an aspen and started prepping the hoof. The foot was long and smooth and shiny and hard like hooves get on new grass. Lester followed me to the tree.

"I still don't see why once we dump the watch, we can't call the family first," he said.

I just pointed to the corral and went back to shoeing.

Lester put his headphones on and caught himself a big bay mare to do the same thing. It wasn't long until that old witch pulled back while Lester was digging in his box for his nippers and knocked him into the dirt. I pointed to his ear, and he pulled out the wires.

"You can't hear that sow, you lose your advantage."

He just grinned and got up.

"The old whore-bucket never touched me," he said. He put the headphones back on, then fiddled with the thing in his pocket, talking in a fake whisper. "But I'll turn it down real low so you won't worry about me none."

We quit about four and had a beer then piled into my old truck. Lester wanted to see Callie and talk high finance before her shift started at the Sierra Peaks, so after we showered up I pointed us down the mountain again.

"Last time I summered up here we'd go a week sometimes between trips to town."

"Yes, old son," Lester said, "but Harvey and May and Albert were all up here then and we had three squares a day and I didn't know Callie Dean. Is it my fault Harvey Linderman wants to be the goddamn Colonel Sanders of the eastern Sierra and franchise this pack outfit to Power Line Creek years after it and Summers Lake and all the other pack outfits in the valley go bust?"

"We're spending a fortune in diesel, bud."

He just grinned and put his headphones on. "Fuel is high, but so am I."

"It must be great to be in love. She even got you off Copenhagen."

He said something back to that but by then we were rattling over the cattle guard on the point of the hill and I couldn't make it out.

When we got to the cabin at the lake Callie was sitting in her bra and some slacks working on the computer and putting on makeup at the same time.

"What's shaking, beautiful?" Lester asked.

"Doing some homework," she said. "The billionaire's son is named Gerald, middle name Quinn, but after he had a falling out with his dad down in Miami he goes by Jerry Q or GQ." She looked up happy like this all made sense. "Like the magazine, you know? He won't use his family name. Since his daddy has all these aviation records in planes and balloons, the boy made a name for himself as a helicopter pilot." She scrolled around some more.

"From the Internet sign I cut last night, he tried to make a name for himself as a dope smuggler too."

Callie shot me a look for that. "No way."

"Got himself arrested for flying marijuana into Key West back when he was nineteen, and his dad had to lawyer him out of the mess."

"Anyway, Mister Preacher," she said, "I found something on the wife trying to get the husband declared dead. It mentioned a Beverly Hills law firm, so here's their number." She held up a piece of paper. "I called four-one-one so you boys can phone her up. Hit the lottery in the cosmic jackpot. And here's the number of Club Tiburón, the son's hangout in a place called South Beach." She smiled right at me. "I got the name from his Facebook wall like he just can't wait for us to call. Now look at this." She got to some personal site that showed this Jerry Q with some big-boobed girls outside a nightclub.

"A lady on cable said GQ is the cowboy in the family," Callie said.

Lester laughed at that. The video showed the same guy I'd seen in the same stupid hat wearing a Hawaiian shirt.

"What a fruit bat," Lester said. "Lookit them baggy pants. And pointy-toed boots he probably bought off some dead Mexican. Cowboy my ass."

Callie walked over to the dinner table and punched a button on the house phone message machine.

"Hey, babe," some guy said, "no veal picata tonight since . . ." She skipped to the next message. It was the lady in Palo Alto that owned the house reminding Callie about the propane delivery.

"Who's calling you 'babe'?" Lester asked.

"Ed," she said. "My boss?"

Lester gave her a sour look. She was punching in numbers on the phone just ignoring him.

"So who you calling . . . babe?" Lester asked.

"Wilshire Boulevard, Beverly Hills," she said, kind of smirky.

"Jesus, Callie, this ain't some high-school crap."

She shushed me and asked whoever answered the phone for the lawyer handling the missing billionaire's wife.

". . . well if you would please tell him that Callie Dean of Piute Meadows, California, has information on the location of her husband's plane. That's right, the location of the crash. Yes, Callie Dean. They can reach me at this number. Thank you."

I stood up and got myself a beer from the fridge.

"Damn, girl. What are you thinking?"

"Now Tommy, by the time these lawyers get back to me, you boys will have returned the watch and called the sheriff. All I'm doing is establishing a time line. Like a record. So if there is any kind of reward from anyone, they'll know it was us had the skinny before the sheriff even knew. You heard me. I played it cool. Never mentioned a reward. Just tried to sound like a concerned citizen."

"I told you she was a smart one," Lester said.

"What time is it, Les?" she asked.

He looked down at that watch. "Four forty-six."

"Damn," she said. "I gotta run." She scampered up the stairs.

Lester sat at the dinner table and watched her go. "What you need to do, old son," he said, "is develop a sense of humor about all this." He picked up the phone and just sort of stared at it. "This is once-in-a-lifetime stuff. When do you think something like this will pass our way again? We got this little secret that's all ours. Let's play this smart

50

and see where it goes." He punched the message button. "What could go wrong?"

"Hey, babe, no veal picata tonight. You can do some sort of chicken picata if you think you have to . . ."

Lester clicked it off. Before I knew it he was punching in numbers himself, looking at Callie's scrap of paper. At first I thought he was calling Ed at the Sierra Peaks to make an idiot of himself.

"Yeah," I heard Lester say after a pause, "Club Tiburón? Is this where that Jerry Q hangs?" He looked over at me and laughed like we were making prank calls in grammar school. Like, is your refrigerator running, sir? Well you best go catch it.

"Oh yeah," Lester said, "Jerry Q." His voice changed then. "Yessir. That's right, Mister Q. My name is Lester Wendover, and I found your dad's plane."

I sat up sharp, just listening to this nonsense. There wasn't much else to do.

"That's right. Me and my partner Tom Smith found the wreck just short of North Pass. That's in California, on the east side of the Sierra. Right, just as plain as day. At the head of Aspen Canyon west from Piute Meadows, then up the north fork. You know where that is? Nosir. About two hours drive south of Reno. No, we didn't tell nobody yet. Thought you should be the first to know. No. We only found it yesterday, and we been trying to track you down." Lester looked over at me as serious as I'd ever seen him. The guy on the phone must have been doing more talking than Lester. That was a switch.

Callie came down the stairs dressed for work. I nodded toward Lester, and she sat next to me and listened.

"Yessir. It was . . . intact. That's right. A positive ID shouldn't be a problem if that's what's worrying—"

Lester put his hand over the phone and whispered loud to us. "He got interrupted. He's yelling at some Mexicans. It's all in Spanish." Lester went back to listening.

I got up and walked out to the deck and just grabbed the railing and held on for a minute. Lester was still sucking up when I came back in, but at least I didn't hear him use my name again.

"Okay, okay. That's right, drive south from Reno. They got car rentals right there at the airport. Sure. You can leave me a message right here at this phone. We got zero cell service up here. Right. Well you're surely welcome. Look forward to it. So long."

Lester paused a bit, then hung up. He didn't say anything for a minute, then he whooped as loud as he did the one time he tried bull-riding down at Bishop when we were seventeen and he lied about his age to make the entry and a gruella bull named Border Patrol bucked him damn near over the chute.

"That was him," Lester said. "Damn. He was right there in that club. I just figured I'd see if they know him, but he was right there in the club next to the damn phone."

"Well you surely played him like a trout on a line, bud. Jesus, Lester, you gave him everything but your mother's maiden name and your social security number."

"So?" he said. "I sure enough got his attention." He got that cocky look. "I bet he's running some pretty big numbers in that rich boy head of his right now."

"And you're not?"

"Wow," Callie said. "This is so cool. But from what we saw, he's going to be pissed we found the plane." She kissed Lester good-bye and picked up her purse. "He might pay us not to tell." She gave me a what-do-you-think-about-that look. "Come by the restaurant later and let's talk this out. I can't wait to meet this Jerry Q. He's a hottie and he is rich." She kissed Lester again like he was rich too. I watched her head for the door.

"Well you two have wound the clock on this now, for sure."

Callie just laughed and ran out to her Nissan, fired it up, and drove off down the dirt drive that circled toward the lake road. We watched that black car bob through the aspen, then get lost in the glare of late sun on the water as she turned toward town.

Chapter Four

We followed Callie into Piute Meadows about six. Lester was quiet for a time. It always galled him when she talked about other guys that way, or when guys like her boss talked flirty with her. He put a boot up on the dash.

"What you need to do," he said, "is trade this damn truck in for something newer. No wonder you haven't got a girl."

"Think that would do it?"

"Why sure. I know this old Dodge Ram was hot stuff when we were in high school, 'Oooh, Tommy's got a winch on his bumper,' but you could go to Fallon Auto Mall and get a teeny-bit-used Ram four-by-four—Cummins and all." He pulled his boot off my dash. "Ram Tough," he said like the old commercials. "Damn truck's older than you are."

"Least it's paid for."

He knew I'd seen the pink overdue notices for his Ford all over the trailer where we bunked. "Well, there is that," he said.

There wasn't much traffic on the lake road. I checked out every car and truck coming my way like a bad habit.

"I surely would have liked it better if he'd just had a suitcase full of cash in that airplane," Lester said when we were about a mile from town, "or a bag full of dope."

"What the hell would you do with a bag full of dope?"

"I'd sell that sucker," he said.

"You'd get yourself shot the first ten minutes."

He was quiet again until I parked behind the Sierra Peaks. He didn't get out of the truck right away. A white sheriff's cruiser was parked across the lot next to Albert Coffey's beat-up Firebird.

"Old GQ should be here in a couple of days," he said. "So even if we report the crash to the sheriff, he knows we're his boys."

"Not if, Lester. When."

"That's what I meant," he said. "All I'm saying is we're going to be in solid with this guy."

"What else did he ask you?"

"He asked what else we found. Like any personal stuff."

"What'd you tell him?"

"That we didn't find a thing," he said. "Just the body with the clothes blowing around. That sort of stuff. He seemed glad his old man wasn't just a couple of bones scattered all over the mountain."

"He said that?"

"Yeah," Lester said. "Exactly that."

"Well, the County will fly the body out as soon as we tell the sheriff. He'll have his daddy back in one piece, then that'll be that."

Lester just grinned like that wouldn't be that. We went in for drinks and dinner.

There were a few Dominion cowboys at the bar. We nodded and said hi and they said hi back, but they tended to keep to themselves. They looked more serious than usual. Ed was behind the bar. I said hi to him too, but Lester didn't. We could see Sarah Cathcart sitting in the dining room with Tony Aguilar. She was in uniform packing her automatic, her handcuffs, and full rig, but she still looked as pretty as she did when she was college rodeo barrel-racing champ and I was in the ninth grade. It must have been her cruiser parked out back. Lester stopped at their table to give her a hard time.

"Hi, Les," she said.

"Hey deputy," he said, "hot date with the silver-haired devil?"

"Not quite," Sarah said.

"I wish," Tony said. "Sarah called me for a medevac this afternoon." He put his hand on his heart. "Three years up here and she don't give me the time of day unless somebody's lost or dying." He leaned forward toward us, but pointed to her. "Such dangerous curves and me with no brakes." He had just the teensiest accent.

We semi-laughed. Sarah looked like she had heard it all before.

"Austin Lambert had a bronc go over with him in the Dominion sorting pens," Sarah said. "Knocked him cold and broke his pelvis in two places. Tony flew him to Reno."

"That explains why his pals look so sour," Lester said.

"Have you boys been out there since Dominion bought the place from Allison's?" Tony asked. "New barn, new bunkhouse with a flatscreen, new corrals. Pretty serious cash outlay. I guess those that have it, spend it." He sipped a big Scotch.

"Investment, Tony," Lester said, "that's the name of the game. Hell, you sound like maybe you'll quit the chopper business and go to buckarooin' for Dominion."

Even Sarah had to smile at that picture.

"They've got no buckaroos out there," she said, "only cowboys."

"Yeah, it's no Flying W." Lester grinned over at me. "That's for sure."

Sarah started back in on her salad, then turned and looked right up at me.

"You're awfully quiet tonight, Tommy."

"Long day, is all. I'm just trying to figure how old Tony could keep his tennis tan under a Stetson and chinks."

She laughed, but looked like she expected me to say more. I grabbed Lester's arm and dragged him to a booth.

"We'll catch you two lovebirds later," he said.

We sat down and ordered a couple of Crown Royals and rib eyes from Judy Burmeister without looking at the menu.

"What's galling you?" Lester asked.

"Sarah. I never felt antsy around the law before. Like I had something to hide. I don't like the feeling."

"Oh," he said, "I thought you were just pissed that Tony was beating your time."

"She's just like a big sister and you know it. She's been listening to your kind of flirty nonsense her whole life. She ain't going to hear any of it from me."

"Easy big fella," he said. "We got nothing to hide. We found a wreck. We're going to let the right folks know." He grabbed some garlic bread. "You worry too much." He ate some bread. "She likes those slick old foreign devils, though. Got no time for us young packers. Remember that French ski instructor?" He studied Sarah across the room. "You ever notice she wears her hair up when she's on duty, but when she's out with some handsome rascal like Tony that palomino hair is hanging down as pretty as a damn rodeo queen?"

"No shit, Lester."

"That girl knows what she's got going on," he said. "Tony must make some serious coin. You know what a chopper-jockey charges per hour for a medevac."

"It ain't like he works every day. I bet the busiest he was all winter was the week he and everybody else was looking for the billionaire, and that was before Christmas."

"He owns his own business, pard," Lester said. He was watching Judy give Sarah and Tony their check. "Women love that." He shoved the bread basket at me and tried to talk with Tony's accent. "Black Label, baby, and hold the ice."

"When he started, he had a second chopper and a second pilot on payroll."

"Times are hard," he said.

Callie came out from the kitchen to bring us our steaks herself. She slid into the booth next to Lester and slipped her arm through his.

"Hey girl," he said, "you're interfering with my eating."

"That'll be the day."

"Thank you, Tommy," she said.

We dug into our food. Say what you want about her, that girl could cook. We all looked over when Sarah and Tony got up after splitting the check. He left through the bar. She came over and sat in the booth next to me.

"So Sarah," Lester said, "any excitement us citizens should know about?"

"Not unless you're Austin Lambert," she said.

Lester looked like he was about to burst, but Sarah wasn't paying him any mind. She looked over at me again.

"My dad's got a three-year-old colt just shipped down from Idaho and needs someone good to start him," she said. "When he heard you were back, he asked me if I thought you'd have the time."

"I'd like that. I'll just need to tell Harvey."

"I'll talk to him," she said. "I'm giving Albert Coffey a ride back up to Power Line Creek at sunup tomorrow to make sure he gets there."

"Good enough. I'd like that a lot."

"Figured you would." She kissed me on the cheek and got up. Callie and Lester waited until she was halfway through the bar before they gave me the old woo-woo. I didn't really mind. I was sort of giving me the old woo-woo myself.

* * *

We had our horses grained and saddled and were inside finishing our breakfast about six-thirty the next day, when we heard a pickup. I looked out the window of the trailer.

"Damn. Run and catch us a packhorse, Lester. Saddle him quick."

"Why?" he said. "It's just Harv."

"Because we lied to him about having trail to fix, is why. Remember? Best gather some tools. Shit."

"I keep telling you Tommy," he said, "quit worrying." But he got up fast and shinnied out to the corral with a halter and snagged a big gray standing close to the fence. He was adjusting the britchen on the pack saddle by the time Harvey got out of the truck.

"Jay-sus Chroist," Harvey said, "ain't you boys left yet?"

"Hell, Harv," Lester said, "we were waiting on you. Thought you'd like to ride up with us. May said a little of that shovel work would slim down that tummy of yours."

Harvey just grunted, but I could see he was half-smiling. He'd take a lot of ribbing from Lester. He pulled a cardboard box from the bed of the truck.

"Got you this alternator," he said, and walked over to the generator parked under some aspens. He lit a Winston and stared at the thing, then set the box in the dirt.

Lester went to help him while I got some pack bags out of the storage trailer we used as a tack room. They drained the big glass bulb on the fuel filter and blew out the fuel line and did all sorts of other nonsense putting in the new alternator. After I packed the tools in the bags and laid out a tarp and lashrope, I went to work with a hammer and spikes fixing corral poles for a bit. I was sitting at our plank table outside the trailer riveting a new strap on a pack bag when I heard the generator fire up. Harvey came around the trailer wiping his hands, then sat down across the table and lit another smoke. I nodded a well-done, but didn't say anything. The generator was like an F-16 taking off. Our three horses stood at the long hitching rack sort of dozing, ignoring the noise.

"I ran into Sarah on the way here," Harvey said loud. "She's going to bring you that colt of her dad's. She's going to pay me board. I told her she didn't need to. That you'd use it as a lead horse before long, but she wanted to give me money. You know Sarah."

"Yeah, that's Sarah."

"I got a box of groceries for you from May," he said. "Ought to last you a week or so." He looked down past the hitching rack where Lester was bringing up the box. Lester had a lot a hustle when it came to groceries. Harvey stood up, stuck his smoke in his mouth, and scratched his belly.

"If you boys are going to fix trail today you better rattle your hocks." He grinned. "Albert's back shoeing mules, so you two are off the hook for a few days. Next time you come up to eat, maybe one of you can drive Albert's Pontiac up for him."

"Sure thing. Thank May for us for the groceries."

He headed back to the truck and drove off as Lester stowed the food, eating cookies out of the bag.

"So you're sure you want me to take back this fine Rolex?" Lester asked.

"Don't start."

"The guy will be here in another day or so and a watch might be the last thing he's even thinking about," he said. "Then if he does mention it, we can tell him we just took it for safekeeping. Then nobody'd know different."

"Would you believe you?"

"You got me there," he said.

"Just grab your gear. A body robber is the worst form of human on the planet. You don't want to be known as one."

We buckled on our chinks and spurs, and were packed and horseback ten minutes later. It was already closer to noon than breakfast.

We hit a long trot to get us out of the Jeffrey pine, kicking up dust as we went. We slowed to a walk on a rise above the creek, and Lester took the pack horse for a while. It was warm for June, but a little breeze kept it about perfect. I was glad we were almost done with this escapade.

"So how come you didn't ride for Dominion when you heard they'd bought Allison's?" Lester asked all of a sudden.

"Harvey asked me to pack up here with your sorry ass while he tried to get the place on Power Line Creek cranked up. Can't say no to Harvey and May."

"You don't want to pack your whole life," he said, "that's what you always told me."

"So?"

"So just I wondered why a well-traveled buckaroo like yourself wouldn't ride for Dominion," he said. "Be cow boss or something."

"Still might. I thought one last season in Aspen Canyon sounded pretty good, though. Like turning back the clock. And a damn sight less corporate. Thought I'd keep you out of trouble. Shows what I know."

"Oh, right," he said.

"If you think Dominion Land and Livestock is such a hot ticket, why don't you work for 'em?"

"Maybe I will," he said, but he looked like he wasn't going anywhere. "They pay better than Harvey."

"You'll need that if you're going to marry Callie Dean."

He laughed out loud. We were climbing through some sagebrush past the second drift fence and got a nose-full of that good sage and dust smell. It grew up to the top of the rock ridge on our right side. Off to our left across the first meadow here was big timber on the ridge that spilled down in front of us across the whole canyon. In a week or so the first cows and calves would be herded up here to graze for the summer. The sky shimmered over the jaggedy peaks at the canyon head.

"So you told Callie you only use my full name to piss me off," he said.

"I was just kidding her. She has the contrary notion you're something special, so it's easy to get her goat."

He liked hearing that.

"Actually, I said it's a good name and your dad gave it to you and you ought to be proud of it."

"I guess this Jerry Q isn't so proud of his old man's name," Lester said.

"Seems like."

"Okay," he said, "what's the best thing your dad gave you?"

"This slick-fork Franklin saddle with a 3-B Visalia tree and his old Remington two-seventy."

"I bet you shot better guns," he said.

"But not nicer ones."

"What else he give you?"

"My good name. That's about all we start out with, I guess."

"You miss him?" he asked.

"All the damn time."

Chapter Five

We left the last meadow and wound through shady pine, fallen timber, bogs, and aspen thickets, then broke out onto the loose shale of The Roughs. We cleared the shale and the trail narrowed then we disappeared into the trees.

It was another hour before we left the tamarack above the forks and started climbing around the outer rim of the cirque and got in sight of the plane. We both knew that something was wrong as soon as we saw it. We kept on riding past the avalanche site until we could get some altitude for a closer look. We stopped the horses after a bit and I pulled out my rifle scope. There was no mistake now that we knew what to look for. I handed the scope to Lester. He stared through it for just a second then handed it back.

"The hell?" he said.

"The body's gone."

"Shit-fire," he said. "How?"

I stowed the scope and we made tracks for the bottom of the snowfield, clattering through the rocks with the mahogany scratching on the leather of our chinks. The snow had melted some in only the two days since we'd ridden there. I pulled up at the whitebark pines and swung off. We tied up and loosened our cinches. Since we never did plan on working trail, the load on the packhorse was so light we left him packed. Neither of us said a word. It just felt like doom up there.

Lester pulled a shovel off the pack on the big gray to carry with him. We started tramping up through the snowfield in our own tracks like before. Lester used the shovel like a long ice axe, but it didn't stop him from slipping and falling a couple of times on the frozen places. The closer we got, the more we could see that things weren't the same.

The body was gone and all the clothes had been picked up. The spot the body had sat on had been raked off and fluffed up with sand and pine duff to cover the ooze the corpse had left when it started thawing. Even the boxer shorts were snatched from the tree. Lester made a move for the cockpit, but I motioned for him to stay back and not touch a thing.

"Somebody's been here. Might still be."

He nodded. I walked around the wreck just looking, trying to remember how it was. Lester held that shovel like he was ready to smack somebody with the blade if they made a move on him.

"You figure somebody took him?" he asked.

"He didn't just up and walk off. Even with his boxers."

"Could it have been a critter? A bear, maybe?"

"I wouldn't want to meet the bear who could make that old boy vanish without a trace."

Lester bent over and looked into the cockpit through the windshield. "Well this looks about the same," he said.

I was looking down through the door. "Nope. Somebody wiped the blood off the instrument panel."

"Then I bet his wallet's gone, too," he said.

"Without going inside I can't tell."

"Damn," he said. "Let's just look."

"Hold off a minute."

I walked around the patch of grass. The ground up that high is just crumbly granite, even where stuff is growing. And in those spots it's soft. There were plenty of footprints if you got low enough to the ground to see them. Lester watched me on my hands and knees like I was a crazy man, but he'd seen me do that before when we were hunting.

"What you got?" he asked.

"Couple of guys besides us. Now look here."

He came over and I showed him the two ruts that helicopter skids had made in the new grass. They were pretty faint, but you could see them if you got close.

"County?" he asked.

"Let's hope. This guy had been sitting right where he died for what, about six or seven months. Then he disappears in a single afternoon, less than twenty-four hours after you phone that idiot son of his."

"And he's a chopper guy," Lester said.

"Yeap. He's most definitely a chopper guy."

"It's probably no big deal," Lester said. "Maybe somebody saw the wreck from the air and called it in, or maybe Gerald Q did the right thing and called the sheriff right after I phoned. Maybe it is County and they flew in and took him just like they would have if it'd been us who called."

"Could be."

"Or maybe after I called him, old GQ chartered a jet to Reno, rented himself a chopper, and flew his old man out while we were poking up the trail horseback. The body could be chilling at the coroner's in Reno right now."

"Maybe so."

I put on my riding gloves and went back to the wreck. I pulled open the cockpit door, took off my hat and stuck my head in. The wallet was gone like Lester figured, and the paper sack with the sandwich and cash was gone. There had been a blue windbreaker, and that was gone too. A torn sheet of legal pad paper was stuck inside the windshield with electrician's tape just below the spiderweb crack where the pilot had hit it with his head. It was covered with big printing in ballpoint. I didn't remember it from before.

"Now this crash has been tampered with twice."

"Who before this?" Lester asked.

"You, numbnuts."

He tried to laugh it off.

"I got a bad feeling somebody is fixing to tell a different story than the one we know." I stepped back so Lester could see the note. "Read that."

He leaned in and read it out loud.

Got caught in a downdraft and missed the pass. Shook up and scared but not hurt bad thank God. Just a bump on the noggin. Have plenty of food, water and warm clothes, so don't worry. Will cross North Pass and walk

*out to Little Meadows pack station for help as it looks
to be closest to a paved road on map. Six or seven miles
tops and I can flag down a ride from there. Will call
when I get to nearest town. Don't worry everybody. See
you soon!*

Lester finished reading. "Damn," he said. "A guy
would have to be crazy to want to climb over the pass
and take that Little Meadows trail with all those creek
crossings. Aspen Canyon is longer, but a damn site easier
walk."

"Especially for a dead guy."

"There is that," he said. "Plus that pack station being
closed in the winter. Let's see that again." He reached past
me for the note. I shoved him back.

"Jesus. Don't touch a thing."

I squatted down and poked a stick at nothing in particular. All I could do was just look around that grassy flat
where the missing clothes and the body used to be.

"Why would somebody write a note like that?" Lester
asked. "Did we miss it the first go-round?"

"Nope. And the blood got wiped off to make it look
like he didn't whack himself so hard. To make it look like
he was in shape to walk out to the Sonora Pass road."

"So what's somebody trying to prove?"

"A lie, Lester. A big, felony kind of lie."

"But we know different," he said, "right?"

"We don't know what we know anymore." I picked
up my hat. It was getting on to late afternoon with a nasty
breeze coming over the pass, and we were a long way from

home. "We best stop by Callie's and see if any of them other eighty people you left her number with phoned her."

"I'm getting spooked," he said.

"You should be."

"You worry me, old son," he said. "You're getting that look."

"Yeah, well."

We slipped and slid down the snowfield. At the bottom we cinched up our horses, grabbed that damned pack-horse with the tools, which was another damn lie, and rode back down the trail. I always felt at home up in this country, the wilder the better, which is why I came back. But now that big mountain half scared me to death.

Chapter Six

We rode back not saying a word. Below the forks the trees along the creek gave us shelter from the wind. We dropped altitude traveling at as fast a walk as the rocky ground would let us. The sun was already down behind us and we could just see glimpses of last light skimming the rim of the canyon. We came to the rise where the Forest Service sign marked the end of the Wilderness Area and let the horses rest. We looked out from a natural notch in the rocks down to The Roughs and all of Aspen Canyon spreading out below us like a big chute, spilling all the way past the valley to the piñon hills out in Nevada about twenty miles distant. It was so pretty that for a minute I forgot the mess we were in. Then it just looked like more ground to cover, empty and far from home.

"So who's been looking for him?" Lester asked. We were just hitting the top of the second meadow about half an hour below The Roughs, fairly rattling along. It was coming on dusk with a new half moon dropping down behind us.

"You know. Everybody. The Air Force. Nevada National Guard. County Search and Rescue. Civil Air Patrol. Nevada Department of Public Safety. Santa Claus."

"I mean who wants him found?"

"Every-damn-body. His family and rich fly-boy friends, I guess. His wife."

"So who doesn't want him found?" Lester asked. "The idiot son?"

"He'd be my first guess, but you never know."

"So it could be somebody we don't even know about yet," he said. "Damn. That whole business back there would cost a pile of money," Lester pulled his horse up. "Hiring a helicopter, finding a couple of lowlifes willing to drag a corpse." He kind of laughed. "Take him off that snowy mountain, the old boy will be getting ripe pretty damn quick. The meat'll be falling off the bone like an overdone turkey." He made a face. "What the hell are they going to do with him, anyway?"

"Whatever they were going to do they've already done."

"There's a lot of country back there," Lester said. "They sure found him quick."

"Well you gave the guy everything but the GPS coordinates, for Christ's sake. But whether it was the idiot-stick son or somebody else, they hadn't been to the wreck when the note on the windscreen got wrote. Leastwise they weren't local. Whoever scribbled that only knew the country from what they saw on a map. Otherwise he would have claimed to be heading the easier way east down Aspen Canyon like we're doing."

"Just like I told you he should," Lester said.

"There you go. You're a damn genius. Now let's get going. Be full dark soon."

"We still got some moon," he said. Then he smiled. "A rustler's moon. Besides, the horses know the way."

"They're the only ones left who do."

We screwed down our hats and hit a long trot until the next aspen grove and by then the wind had died. It was another hour before we were poking along the last bit of jeep trail through the sage and moonshadow just above the pack station with the creek racing along below us on the right. I half expected to see Harvey's truck waiting for us in the trees and wondered what the hell I would tell him about where we'd been, but of course the only trucks outside the trailer were Lester's and mine. We unsaddled and turned out the stock. By then we were fried and hungry.

We went inside, and I lit the lamps in the trailer. I stood there in the front room looking things over while Lester took a shower. It wasn't super noticeable, but just enough things were moved around that a person could tell someone had been there and wanted us to know they had. And then there was the smell. On top of the smoke of a fresh-struck wooden match and the almost sweet smell of plain kerosene burning clean in the glass lamps on the table was something different. A thick perfumey stink, but just a leftover hint, and not like anything from a woman. More like some pimp bouncer with gold chains at the Midnight Ranch or the mensroom at a ballgame on a hot day or a barracks on Saturday night when the passes were handed out. I'd already spooked Lester enough and didn't say anything about it right away. While he was still in the shower, I grabbed a flashlight and went out to the tin shack behind the propane tank under the aspens. It was where Lester and I used to bunk a few summers back when Harvey and May lived in the trailer. We used it mostly for storage now, but it'd be packed with deer hunters or extra help come fall. I reached up under some tar paper above the door frame and felt for my deer rifle. It was my dad's good Remington .270, and it was still there in his saddle scabbard. I set the flashlight on an iron bunk and eased the rifle down from where I'd wedged it up between the wall studs. I slid it out of the scabbard and opened the breech, then clicked it shut and ran my hand over the stock. It would be wanting a good oiling, but just holding it made me feel better. I guess it was coming to that. I sat down on the plank porch of the shack with the rifle across my knees, looking out over our horse pasture to the trees above the little bridge in the dark, memorizing the terrain I'd known my whole life. The tin shack had been another snow survey hut built sometime in the fifties to replace the log cabin at the forks. Harvey bought it for surplus about the time I was born, and drug it down from the second meadow with a Cat. It still had the yellow Forest Service sign on the door telling folks in green letters Do Not Molest. It was a little late for that. When I heard Lester coming out of the shower I got up, slipped the rifle back in the scabbard, then stowed it behind the seat of my Dodge and went back inside. After I showered off we drove to town to see Callie Dean.

"So what do we say if this GQ has reported the wreck and we didn't?" Lester asked. I was making the last turn through the pastures.

"He won't just yet."

"But what if he did and then Sarah asks us?"

"Improvise, Lester."

He stared out the window at nothing in particular until we hit the street lights. "I'm hungry as hell," he said then. "God, I hope she hasn't closed the kitchen." He looked over at me like it was our biggest worry in the world. "What time is it, you think?"

"You're the one with the damn watch."

I parked behind the Sierra Peaks next to Albert's Firebird and we went inside. Ed said that Callie had called in sick and that he'd had to close the kitchen early. He didn't seem too pleased. He said he had a couple of spaghetti dinners he could rustle up if we were starving. Lester allowed we sure were. I started in on some Dago red and garlic bread that Judy brought us, while Lester asked Ed if he could use the office phone to call Callie out at the lake. While he was gone, I chewed my bread and watched some fly fishermen talking to Tony Aguilar in the bar. They were dressed like fly fishermen, but the clothes looked like they just bought them from the sporting goods store down the street. They were built more like cops or bodybuilders than businessmen. They seemed to be doing all the talking.

Lester came back quick enough.

"She don't answer," he said. "You think she's alright?"

"Sure."

"You think we should go out there and see?"

"Yeap."

"Then you don't think she's alright," he said.

We dug into our dinners, and were just finishing when Tony stopped by our booth. The fly fishermen were heading out the front door of the bar, laughing.

"Who's your pals?" Lester asked him. "Some sort of Mexicans?" The fishermen were both black-haired and Latin looking.

"They're Cubans," Tony said, like it was something nasty.

"Like I said. Some sort of Mexicans," Lester said. "Kinda like you Argen-tines."

"They asked a bunch of questions about last winter," Tony said, pretty much ignoring Lester. "About the search for that missing plane. Did it extend this far west, that sort of stuff."

Lester sat up. "What's it to them?" he asked, but he was looking at me.

"Flying buddies of the rich one," Tony said. "But from the way they talked, they're no pilots. Just arrogant assholes."

"Flying buddies from the Flying W?"

"Who knows, Tomás." He put a hand on my shoulder. "I better go do my paperwork for the county. At least they pay quicker than rich bastards." He nodded and left through the side door of the restaurant like he didn't want to run into the Cubans.

"You about done?"

"Yeah," said Lester.

"Then let's scoot on out to the lake." We hadn't been in that place for more than twenty minutes.

We were flying past the logging road turnoff to the pack station. I told Lester that somebody had been in the trailer that afternoon before we got back from North Pass.

"What were they after?" he asked. He looked about half sick.

"Us, I figure."

"But they didn't take nothing."

"They were just letting us know they were there. Like a dog pissing on a tree."

"So if they know where we live . . ." He didn't even bother to finish, just stared ahead at the road.

I pushed the truck through the sagebrush curves in the creek canyon, then floored it on the straightaway to the lake.

We parked above the cabin in the trees like always, but Callie's Nissan was gone. When we got out, Lester walked down the dirt drive to where it looped around and you could see it end on the pavement by the water. He looked back like he couldn't believe she wasn't there.

"The hell?" he said.

Inside there was a note from Callie stuck on the refrigerator.

Hello my sweet boys. I got a call from our new best friend Jerry Q. He's coming down from Reno and I'm meeting him up at State Line Lodge. I said I didn't know when you were coming off the mountain and he

*said he wanted to touch base. Boy he's a charmer. Rich
<u>and</u> cute—just my type! Things are moving fast for us.
I'll be late, so don't wait for me. This is very cool. Hasta
mañana vaqueros.*

Love, C

Lester pulled the note from the fridge and just stared
at the paper.

"You think we should drive up there?" he asked.

"Don't you?"

"Shit." He dropped into a chair at the dining room
table. "She should get service out at State Line." He punched
in numbers on the house phone on the table. Then he set
it down. "Straight to voicemail," he said. "Damnit, Tommy
we got hell's own long day ahead of us tomorrow. Fence
to fix. And the yard lights? We already lost today farting
around with the plane. We can't go gallivanting all over the
place, right? What do we tell Harvey?"

"Who are you and what'd you do with Lester
Wendover?"

"Screw you."

"Hell, Lester, calling the idiot-stick was your idea.
Now he's come to Reno. Strange Cubans are in town asking about that plane, and somebody's dogging our tracks.
We got to go. Besides, diesel's cheaper at State Line and I'm
getting low." I pointed to the answering machine. The light
was flashing. "See who's been calling your girl."

He hit the button. The first message was a woman's
voice. She said she was an attorney named Nora Ross from
the Beverly Hills law office representing the dead guy's

wife. She was calling back about Callie's voicemail that we'd found the plane.

". . . this office is naturally interested in any information you might have about her husband's disappearance or the location of his airplane, but inquiries with the Frémont County Sheriff's office indicate that they have no knowledge of such a discovery. Unless verification can be provided, Miss Dean, this office will be forced to regard your message as a hoax, or worse, some sort of an attempt at fraud, which I need to remind you would be actionable. Please call me at . . ."

Then the phone picked up and Callie came on the line. She sounded just as sweet and charming as could be.

"Oh, Miss Ross, it's so good of you to get back to me. Trust me, this is no hoax. My fiancé Les Wendover is a back-country outfitter, and when he found the poor man's body we—that is he—thought the proper thing to do was first to notify your—"

Then the message cut off.

"I wish I knew what she thought she was trying to pull."

Lester just looked sort of numb. "I don't know," he said. "She's just trying to make something happen."

"Girl doesn't know when to shut up."

He pushed the button again, but it was only him, calling from the Sierra Peaks. He killed it before I could hear. Then he stuck the note back on the refrigerator and sort of smoothed it flat like that would put everything back to normal.

81

I stood up and took a long pull from the Crown Royal bottle we'd left a couple of nights before. "Let's go." I started to put the bottle back on the sideboard but decided it might be more useful in the truck.

A bit of moonlight hit the lake ahead of us as I rolled through the aspens down to the pavement. Lester was about as quiet as I ever saw him, so I let him be. If he noticed the half-full box of 150 grain .270 soft points sitting on the dash, he didn't let on or care. We turned left at the north edge of town about ten minutes later, then headed west across the valley toward Dominion headquarters.

"You think GQ's putting the moves on her?" he asked.

"I think he's got other things on his mind. Jesus, Lester, focus. She's one girl that can sure take care of herself in that department."

"I guess," he said. That notion didn't please him much either.

The Reno Highway made a hard right at the old ranch house in the cottonwoods where the Dominion foreman lived, then curved north out of the valley toward Hell Gate Pass. He didn't say another word. After the Sonora turn-off, we were in West Frémont canyon, the road slow and windey through big timber, with the river close by the pavement on our right. We'd catch glimpses of the water flashing when the headlights hit it in a curve and could see the pines rocking in the wind, but no moonlight shone down in the canyon, so mostly it was dark as hell.

I slowed when I saw red lights ahead through the trees. Lester caught me dropping my right hand behind the seat to feel for the rifle. He glanced behind the seat and gave a laugh when he saw what I was reaching for.

"Easy, pard," he said. "Just some fisherman missed a curve. Happens all the time. Remember that gamblers' bus?"

When we got closer, we could see a whole mess of lights. Two sheriff's cruisers, a county ambulance, a Forest Service Suburban, a tow truck, and some stalled traffic. A couple of sheriffs with flares were stopping cars going both ways.

"Shit-fire," Lester said.

I pulled up behind a camper, and we waited as a deputy with a flashlight walked toward us. Ahead of us we could see lights shining out into the stream, and we could make out lines stretching over to a car out in the shallow water. There were a couple of guys in the stream up to their waists hanging on to ropes or cables, looking slick and dark. Probably wetsuits. Lights flashed behind us, and a second ambulance passed us northbound in the southbound lane. I saw Lester's face in the flashing lights. It didn't look good. When the deputy got closer, we saw it was Sarah. She stopped when she saw it was us, only coming as far as the camper just ahead. After a second she jerked her head and walked back up the road to the commotion. We got out and followed her. We were still a ways away when we could see in the spotlights that the car on its side in the river was Callie's black Nissan. I heard all the air and the life go out of Lester in the same second. He hung back like not seeing it up close would make it go away.

"Shit, Tommy," was all he could get through his wind-pipe. He said it a bunch of times.

"Come on." I led him into that mess of people. We stood on the gravel under the pines with the red, blue, and white lights flashing and the radio crosstalk and the rush of the river and some county officers talking and laughing among themselves about something else entirely with their back to the river like nobody had just died, making everything all jumbly and crazed. Lester started breathing deep, and I led him to a big Jeffrey pine and parked him there, letting him watch, kind of hugging himself and rocking back and forth like a hurt kid.

I walked to the Dodge Ram and got the bottle of Crown Royal. I hurried back to the tree and handed it to Lester. He nodded thanks and took a big pull. Then I walked over to find Sarah. I just stood there next to her as the crew in the wetsuits stumbled on the boulders as they fought the current pushing that bubbling water down toward State Line. They were hauling something with ropes from the center of the current and it didn't take much light to guess it was Callie. I glanced back at Lester, but he wasn't watching. He was plugging in his headphones and fiddling with the screen on his phone. He took another pull on the Crown Royal and looked to be talking to himself.

When I looked back at Sarah, she was studying me. It always made me feel funny when she'd do that. She gave her head a little nod and walked away from the water's edge.

"So tell me where Callie was heading after she called in sick."

Sarah had already done some legwork, and there was no telling how much she knew. She wasn't about to give me a hint.

"Don't know."

She looked around at the crowd of cars and trucks and lights. "But you're here, Tommy. Right on her trail." She put her hand on my arm. "You always found what you were tracking. That's what my dad said. Even if it was gutshot or busted-legged and dead when you caught up with it. So why were you trailing Callie Dean?"

After a second or two when I had no kind of answer, I figured I'd try a lie. If I kept at it, I had to get better at telling one.

"Lovers' quarrel?"

She made a bullshit sort of sound. I suppose if I didn't believe it there was no reason she should.

"Right now," she said, "it looks like a single car accident. Driver's error. She was probably in a hurry to get somewhere"—she looked me right in the eye—"or away from somewhere, hit a turn too fast, spun out, and flipped into the river." She turned to the crew attaching cables in the water. "Happens all the time." She looked back at me. "You know that."

"I do."

"I just wish you'd tell me what else you know," she said.

"Old Callie always had a wild streak, I guess."

"Well, that streak ran out tonight."

"Yeah."

"Yeah," she said. "Yeah. Don't scamper off just yet." She left me there and walked back to the bank where they were dragging the body out of the water. I walked over to where Lester was holding up the tree. He kept his eyes on the river but handed me the bottle. I took a drink and handed it back. He made a big sigh and tried to say something that half sounded like why did this have to happen to her just when things were about to come our way. He'd sob then choke it back and try to talk some more.

"You about ready to go home?"

He nodded yeah.

"Nothing we can do here."

He nodded again.

"You sit tight, and I'll go tell Sarah we're leaving." There's just nothing to say to a person.

The ambulance crew was getting the body squared away on a gurney when I got there. An EMT was checking it over, while half a dozen folks watched. I was the only one who wasn't in uniform, so I hung back and let them do their job. Callie was wearing what was left of a short little dress. She had pretty outstanding legs and liked to show them off when she wasn't at work. I guess she wanted to catch Gerald Q's eye. If she'd been wearing shoes or underpants, they'd been torn off by the current and would show up in Tiny Arriella's alfalfa field in Hudson Valley by the end of July. They rolled her back and forth on the gurney, writing down injuries. She had a tramp-stamp across the top of her butt, a Chinese-looking tattoo that a boyfriend could read if she was in the right position, and if he understood Chinese. Lester had never bragged about it, so she must have had it before they ever met. Her skin looked blue-white in the spotlights.

After Sarah officially identified the body, she sidled over, slipped her arm in mine, and walked me away from that mess like we were at a dance.

"We're trying to sort this out," she said. "Callie called Ed at the Sierra Peaks around four o'clock to say she wasn't feeling well enough to come to work. But when Judy Burmeister shows up to waitress at six, she sees Callie talking to somebody in the Hunters' Lodge parking lot across the street. Judy didn't tell Ed 'cause she didn't want to get Callie in trouble, but she told me."

"So who was she talking to?"

"Some city guy in an expensive car," she said.

"Oh that narrows it down."

"Don't be a smartass, Tommy. Your girlfriend is dead."

I nodded over to Lester under the tree. "His girlfriend."

"She was your friend, too." Sarah looked about as pissed off at me as I'd ever seen her. She described the guy Judy said Callie had been talking to. It sounded like one of the Cuban fly fisherman we'd seen a few hours earlier. Sarah looked at her watch.

"It's almost eleven now," she said. "The crew figures by body temp she's been in the water two to three hours. So she leaves Piute Meadows at say seven thirty and loses control at eight. Just about dark. Did Les hear from her between four and eight?"

"Nope. He was with me, and we were just coming out of Aspen so she couldn't have reached him. Didn't get back to the pack station till after dark."

Sarah looked truly surprised. "You had a trip today?"

"Nope. Just fixing trail."

She looked at me the way my mother used to when I'd been out partying in high school and came home stinking of Coors. She poked me in the chest.

"But you're here now and you won't say why." She looked over at Lester. "Great. Get him out of here," she said, "just go." She walked away, pissed as hell.

Chapter Seven

I got Lester led halfway back to my Dodge when he pulled away and ran over to the ambulance. They were just buttoning things up, but most of the county people knew Lester and let him through. He took a long look at the body, then gave a halfway nod to the EMT and walked away hugging his arms as hard as he could.

When I was turning the truck around, I asked him if he wanted to go anywhere or see anybody. His folks lived over the mountain in Grass Valley now, and I would have tanked up and driven half the night to get him there if he'd said so. He just mumbled he wanted to go home, so I headed back towards Piute Meadows. The road was empty and dark.

"She called me her fiancé," he said, apropos of not a damn thing when I pulled into the Shell station in town about twenty minutes later.

When we rattled over the little bridge below the pack station about twenty minutes after that, the Crown

Royal bottle was clanking on the floorboards and he was passed out. I walked him into the trailer and dropped him on his bed. I pulled off his boots and threw a blanket over him. There wasn't much I could do for him after that till hangover time at sunup.

I walked back outside. I took the rifle scabbard and box of cartridges from the truck and sat back on the porch of the tin shack. It was a good spot, a bit off to the side of the trailer in the trees and the little bit of yellow light from the kerosene lamps inside the trailer didn't reach it. It gave me a good view of the dirt road winding toward me through the aspen from the bridge and of the hill across the creek where the road dropped down to the meadow. I took a beer and the tacklebox with my cleaning kit from the trailer and sat back down. Then I gave the Remington a good cleaning and oiling, taking my time, pulling the bolt and setting it down on a piece of newspaper next to me, feeling every part there in the dark without even trying to look at it. I was out there a long time, just enjoying the night, studying the dark line of trees in the half-moonlight. When I was finished, and I'd wiped down the action and polished the walnut stock with a clean rag and rubbed the leather sling with glycerin soap, I loaded the magazine with the soft tips and slid the bolt shut. I found a rusty metal lawnchair with springs that Harvey'd left under a tree, brushed the dead leaves off the seat and set it on the porch. I sort of dozed there in the chair with the loaded rifle across my lap for half the night. I remember the moon was down when I woke one time, and it was cold. Finally, I got restless and got up. I cradled the rifle in my arm and went walking along the curving dirt road through the aspen down to the bridge with the morning star low in the east and bright as a jet coming in to land. I sat in the sagebrush with my back against a rock and studied the bridge in the dark. It was nothing but the undercarriage of an old railroad freight car, just two big I-beams with steel plate and planks over it and no railings, not even a bit of board to tell you if your wheels were going off the edge. How the hell Harvey got it up the logging road and down into the canyon is anybody's guess, but it had been there for as long as I'd been coming here. I remember the first time I drove Harvey's stock truck over it when I was sixteen and you couldn't see the edge of the bridge from the cab it was so narrow. Harv laughed like hell as I tried to look down. He told me to keep my eye on the far bank and the nose of the truck heading straight down the center of the bridge, and we wouldn't fall eight feet over on our side in the cold water with six really surprised mules.

Above the bridge the road climbed a cut to the trailhead. Just past the rise on the right there was a locked aluminum gate that kept the backpackers' cars from going any further up the south side of the canyon. Only the Forest Service, Harvey, and Bonner and Tyree, who held the grazing permit, had keys.

When the first hint of gray showed down-canyon, I rousted myself and walked back to the trailer in the sweet dawn. There was no breeze in the early morning, and the quaking aspen leaves were as quiet as church. Lester was still snoring away. I covered him with another blanket, blew out the lamps, and crawled into my bedroll in the front room to catch a couple of hours downtime.

By late morning I'd fed Lester some aspirin, a big ome-let with Tabasco, bacon, coffee and a beer, and we'd talked some. Outside I started stringing electric line for the yard lights we'd be needing come deer season. I hooked up a big spotlight above the loading chute first. I kept the rifle in the scabbard nearby just out of habit while I worked and slung it over my shoulder when I walked away from the corrals. I was running wire from the generator down through the aspen outside the pasture fence when I saw Sarah's rig mak-ing the turn above the bridge. I could see there was a horse in her trailer. She stopped when she saw me step out of the trees right in front of her, the rifle resting across my shoulder like a baseball bat. Sarah just looked at me as I walked past the cab of her pickup, took a foothold by the trailer wheel well, and swung up. She eased the rig on down the road and I looked in at the horse. It was a big sorrel colt and didn't pay me any mind. I skipped off the trailer as Sarah circled the rig and parked next to our horse corral. I waited for her to get out. She wasn't in uniform, just Wranglers, ropers, a tanktop, and shades, which is uniform enough. She watched me slip the rifle into the scabbard lying in the grain trough of the hitching rack before I unlatched the trailer gate.

"Expecting trouble?" she asked.

"You were so pissed at me last night I thought I'd best protect myself."

She gave me a dirty look, and we unloaded the colt. He was a bit snorty at the new place, but he settled in when I put him in the holding pen by the chute with a flake of hay. He challenged a couple of our knotheads at the corral fence, then set to eating.

"Dad really appreciates this," she said. She handed me three one hundred dollar bills.

"That's too much."

"You haven't got on him yet," she said. "This'll get you started."

Lester stepped out of our trailer to see what was going on and sat on the steps wearing his shades, nursing a beer. He put his headphones on and went to listening to music, not looking at us.

"How's your partner in crime?" she asked.

"He's thrashed, but he'll get over it."

Sarah walked over to the hitching rack where I'd set the rifle. "You must be a mind reader," she said, tapping her finger on the scabbard leather. "We had a team all over the crash site this morning. There was a second set of tire marks."

"Head on?"

She shook her head. "Same direction. And there were fresh paint scrapes on the driver's side of her car. So it looks like somebody forced her off the road." She studied me that way she did. "It could be an accident, maybe some drunk just trying to pass on a curve and running out of room or nerve. Or it could be intentional." She flicked her fingernail against the scabbard again. "But you're not surprised, are you, Tommy. You obviously think that's a possibility."

I just let her talk. As soon as she said that, I knew somebody killed Callie Dean for the lies we told.

"Right now, bare minimum, we're treating it as felony hit-and-run," she said. "We're sending paint scrapings to the lab in Sacramento."

"Okay."

"You don't give anything up, do you? Mister name-rank-and-serial number."

"Them's the rules."

"She didn't die right away, Tommy. Her neck was broken, but she drowned, probably still conscious. Not a fun way to go."

When I didn't say anything, she picked up the scabbard and slid out the .270.

"It's loaded."

"I wouldn't expect any less from you," she said. She held the rifle like a pro but kept her hands off the bolt. She slid it back in the scabbard and set it down real easy in the grain trough like she found it. "I remember your dad hunting with that rifle with my dad," she said.

"What else is on your mind, Sarah?" She was making me uncomfortable as hell.

"We found crystal meth in a ziplock bag in Callie's car," she said.

"Girl had her faults. You know, like being a nymphomaniac and all, but she wasn't no tweaker."

Sarah looked over at Lester sitting on the steps. "Boy," she said, "a girl would have to be a nymphomaniac."

"I thought all you ladies loved Lester."

"Les is a child," she said.

"He's almost the same age as me."

"You're the wise old man, Tommy. You were born that way." She looked at me kind of cranky. "What—you don't think I know exactly how old you are?"

"Well, I don't feel so wise right about now."

"No," she said, "I guess you don't." She just stared at Lester on the porch. "If it's any consolation, I don't think she was a tweaker either. Callie was too vain to trash her looks." She thought about things for a minute. "If she were using that garbage she would have had her stuff handy, loose and careless like they do, not double sealed in two ziplocks. Somebody wanted it to survive a couple of hours in the river."

"Yeah. That'd be whoever killed her. You going to check the cabin? Probably some planted there too."

"We are," she said. "What I'd like to know is how you figured out it was no accident before I told you. I sure wish I knew what you scamps were up to. You're the most unparanoid man I know, but you're walking around with a loaded firearm before lunch and won't say why."

I just kind of shrugged like I did that sort of thing every day.

"So you're not going to let me know where Callie was going?" she asked.

"Girl didn't tell me her deep thoughts."

"Fair enough," she said. "Have Les come in to see me when he straightens up. He'll tell me what I need to know. He never could keep a secret."

"Yes ma'am."

She finally smiled a bit at that, which was a relief. She got back in the truck, started the engine, and rolled down the window.

"And when you see Harvey, ask him to have Albert come see me too."

"Albert?"

"The department got a cockamamie e-mail from some guy in Florida," she said, "the son of that flyer who disappeared before Christmas. This guy said one of his employees just found a record of a phone call from some drunken guy named Albert from our area code."

"Well that's just a few thousand square miles."

"I know," she said. "But this guy thinks his dad survived and said that this 'Albert' was talking crazy and claimed to have seen him alive back then. He says he's contacted every law enforcement agency on the map."

"So how many drunken Alberts in our area code, you figure?"

She kind of laughed. "Maybe a few. The e-mail said this Albert told them he gave somebody who fits the missing guy's profile a ride out from Sonora Junction by Little Meadows pack station up to State Line about the time the plane went down."

"So why tell me?"

"'Cause you work with him?" She gave me a look fit for idiots, which I deserved. "Just have him come see me, okay?"

"So when did you get this e-mail?"

She got that big sister look then. "I don't know," she said, "yesterday. It's been a busy twenty-four hours. What does it matter?"

"I don't mean to tell you your business, but you may want to check with Mammoth, Bishop, Markleeville, maybe down to Barstow and all them to see if they got the same e-mail like the guy said."

She started looking pissed again. "So you don't want to tell me my business," she said.

"Just do it for shits and grins, Sarah."

"Fine," she said. "Now what is going on?"

"Well. From what she told us, Callie may have contacted that same Florida guy herself." I figured I'd tell her at least that much. If the deputies were out at the house at the lake, they probably heard the phone message and saw her note. "About that plane."

Sarah just shook her head. Both hands were squeezing the steering wheel, which was better than having them wringing my neck, which she looked halfway ready to do.

"Have Albert see me," she said. "Tomorrow when I'm back in the office. Not that he'd remember a phone call he made eight months ago. He usually can't remember where he parked his car."

"Maybe he's having flashbacks."

She looked me over to see if I was kidding. When she saw I wasn't, she kind of softened up.

"When you've got your story straight and are ready to talk about what Callie knew about that stupid plane or whatever she was cooking up, you'd best come see me, too. Don't you go having flashbacks on me, Tommy."

"What happened in Iraq stays in Iraq."

She reached out the window and squeezed my arm. "You let me know if you want any company when you sack out that colt. Dad is sure grateful you're back safe. He always said you put the best start on a horse of anybody around." She rolled up the window, fired up the air conditioning, and drove off into the aspen. I picked up the rifle and went back to stringing electrical like a crazy person.

Chapter Eight

About four I put Lester down for a nap like some puppy and told him I had to run into town. He still wasn't really talking, just trying to maintain. When I was crossing the cattle guard on the point of the hill, I saw Harvey's truck heading up the mountain. I pulled over and waited for him there on a straight stretch of the washboard road in the sagebrush with the whole valley down the slope on my left and fresh mule ear growing along the edge of the road. It was coming on summer alright.

"Well this is a helluva note," he said when he'd pulled up opposite and lit a smoke. "How's Les?"

"Hungover."

"Just as well." He took off his hat and scratched his head. "May wants you boys to come up for supper if you can. Keep his mind off things." I could see about six head of horses in the truck. One of them kicked the slats and Harvey yelled a warning, like they could hear it.

"If you can drag Lester with you now, I'll try to make it, but I was going to run up to Dave Cathcart's in Rickey Junction before dark to talk to him about that colt. If Sarah's off duty, she'll be cooking for her dad." Lies just poured out of me now.

Harvey got that twinkle in his eye. "You'd like to get something cooking with old Sarah," he said.

"Yeah, well, wouldn't we all. What are you up to?"

"Dropping a few more head out on your meadow for the week. No wonder that goddamn Power Line Creek outfit always goes broke feeding hay twice a day with no pasture. I oughtta have my head examined."

Harv put his hat on and put the truck in gear. "I dropped Albert off this morning to pick up his Firebird," he said. "You see him in town, point him back up the hill before he gets a snootful."

"You got it."

"Too damn bad about the girl," he said.

We drove off in opposite directions. When I got to the paved road, I turned right toward the lake, not left to town. I slowed down when I got close to the house, peering up into the aspen with the lake just sparkling on my left. I could see a sheriff's SUV parked up on the drive above the house. There were two new deputies I didn't know very well joking and goofing around by the vehicle. If they'd found any meth planted in the house, it didn't seem to make a hell of an impression. I drove on down the road and stopped at the resort store to pick up a sixpack of Coors to freshen Lester's stash. The deputies were still bullshitting in the aspens when I drove back down the road.

When I got to town about fifteen minutes later, I parked behind the Sierra Peaks. The spot where Albert's Firebird had rested for a week or two was empty, just a smear of motor oil and another of power steering fluid on the dirt like always. Automotive maintenance was never high on Albert's list. I went into the bar to cut for his sign. I wanted to talk to him before Sarah got to him.

"Hey, hon," Judy Burmeister said. The old blond was tending bar with one customer. She seemed pretty down.

"Don't suppose you seen Albert Coffey?"

"Oh yeah," she said. "Hours ago. Albert was getting lucky for a change."

"Some gal from the Frémont Lake Rez?"

"No," she said. "More like the Jimmy Buffet song. She was a beauty, a Mexican cutie."

I already seemed to know where this was going. "What'd she look like?"

"A flirty thirty," she said. "Pouty with a cute hair-cut and bangs and lots of cleavage. He didn't stand a chance."

"Albert's fifty-nine, for god's sake, and tends to drool by the third beer."

"Oh, don't I know it," she said. "But a fat disability check makes 'em all Brad Pitt to us, hon." She set down a draft without me asking.

"Maybe they're across the street," she said, nodding toward the front door. There were two more bars in town, one in the old Mansion House Hotel and one at the Hunter's Lodge.

"Albert's car is gone."

"Well," she said. "The babe told him she was down from State Line Lodge."

"How about that."

"When you see Les," she said, "you give him my love, okay? We're all just as sorry as can be about Callie."

She started to tear up. I downed a courtesy swallow of the draft, left some cash and went outside into the sun. I cruised around town but didn't see the Firebird, but then I didn't expect to. I stopped at the NAPA behind the Mark Twain Café and bought a couple of big switches I'd need to finish the yard lights, then I headed north on the Reno Highway and was winding through the pines along the West Frémont in no time. I pulled over where the Nissan went into the river and got out. The tire tracks Sarah told me about were easy to read once you knew what to look for. I popped one of Lester's Coors and stood there in the middle of the road with the rush of that cold river and the afternoon breeze just ruffling every living thing and the vanilla smell of the Jeffrey pine and Steller's jays buzzing around overhead. I walked along the pavement studying stuff and trying to figure what I'd find if I took the time to drive up to State Line. The cheap diesel over in Nevada would make it worth my while, but I'd have to be paying Harvey pretty soon if I didn't quit this foolishness and get back to work. I could see the big rock in the middle of the water where the Nissan came to rest on its side and where Callie drowned with a broken neck and just enough time and consciousness to figure that nothing she'd dreamed about was ever going to happen. I didn't have to think about how scared she was to die. A bit of broken taillight sat on the asphalt. I poked it with my boot toe but let it lie.

After a few minutes I piled back into the Dodge and headed north. The canyon opened up at the Indian curio shop at the edge of Shoshone Valley with the highway sticking to the mountain edge and pastureland spreading off to the right. At Rickey Junction, I had to slow down for the high school and could see Dave Cathcart's barn across a horse pasture, but cottonwoods hid the house. I caught a glimpse of Sarah's rig parked next to the barn as I cruised by. In a few more miles when the road climbed above the irrigation reservoir, I could look north and see the neon of the State Line Lodge and its Legal Limit Casino in the distance, just over the border in Nevada.

When I pulled into the casino parking lot, a fire truck was pulling out. Another was parked across the lot in front of the guest rooms with personnel in their fireproof canvas pants with tee shirts in the heat. It looked like they'd had a little workout. Water was all over the pavement around the truck and two cruisers from Douglas County, Nevada, were parked alongside. People from the lodge stood around gawking. It was easy to spot Albert's old Firebird. Two deputies were standing next to it, and one was writing in a notebook. I got out and went into the Legal Limit.

Those old casinos all have the same sour beer and cigarette smell in the middle of the day, even when there's no customers except at the bar and no smoking inside anymore. A couple of tourists from California were playing slots, but the joint was pretty dead and I was the only big hat in the place. That made the change girl in shorts and

boots who was old enough to be my mother glance over
at me, then glance away. She sat on a stool staring out the
glass doors to the cops outside. I walked over and stared
out the doors with her. I didn't see any cuties, Mexican or
otherwise, but the woman I was looking for was probably
a Cuban anyway.

"You have a fire?"

"Yeah," the change girl said. "Some Indian was cooking up some meth in one of the rooms and set the drapes
and one of the trees on fire."

"He's dead, I suppose."

She gave me a funny look when I said that.

"Oh yeah," she said. "He's dead alright."

I went outside. The deputies had the Firebird's doors
and trunk open and were poking around inside the car.
The paint was in bad shape, and the big orange bird on the
hood was looking pretty shabby. There was no ambulance,
so Albert's body must have been long gone. I just tried to
look like a curious old waddie to see what they were finding
in his car, but the closest deputy gave me one of those can-
I-help-you-sir looks that says move-along-asshole, so I got
in the Dodge and drove over to the pumps to fill up with
that good cheap diesel. It was getting on toward dusk, and
the lights were already on over the pumps. A guy about ten
years older than me watched me fuel up from the parking
lot, standing close enough to the Firebird to see what the
deputies were finding. They didn't tell him to move along,
and he wasn't taking any hints. He wore a Hawaiian shirt
and baggy pants and Mexican looking boots with silver
tips, but he was no Mexican either. He smiled and waved

just cocky as hell when he caught me watching him. His hair looked oily and slicked back in the yard lights. Even without the stupid hat I recognized him from the computer videos. He sure as hell recognized me. I finished pumping my diesel. When I looked up again the guy was gone. I drove back south to Piute Meadows slow and cautious with my eyes on my rearview mirrors. I figured I was too late for supper with Harvey and May. I didn't want to have to tell them about Albert anyway. I'd let the law do that. With him dead, I sure as hell would be doing more shoeing up there this summer, unless I quit paying attention and ended up the same way.

It was full dark when I got back to town and turned right into the meadows heading home. Course I knew I wasn't going any such place. I was even lying to myself now. Pretty soon I cruised real slow along the lake, looking up to see if there were any cars parked at the cabin. It was dark and the driveway was empty. I pulled over a few hundred yards past it and parked the truck off the pavement in a little opening in the pines. A person couldn't see it from the house at all. Then I walked back through the trees and slipped into the kitchen from the side door off the deck. I turned on a low lamp in the living room and started taking inventory. Callie's note about meeting GQ at State Line was gone from the refrigerator. Whether the deputies or someone else had walked off with it was anybody's guess. I played the answering machine. The message from the lady lawyer was erased, but Lester's was still there. That probably meant it wasn't the deputies who did the erasing.

I went upstairs to the room Callie used. It had the usual girl mess of open drawers, curling irons and underpants on the floor, but nothing more than that. I was scanning the dressertop for any notes or hints when I saw headlights flicker down in the living room. I scooted down the stairs and made it out the kitchen to the side deck about the time I heard a car door close above me on the drive. I was on the opposite side of the house from the wooden steps that came down from the drive to the living room door. Other than the one lamp, I hadn't left anything that would say I was there. I backed down the deck far enough to see that the car up above was a silver Infiniti. I could hear footsteps coming down the stairs. The wood creaked like hell. A light switched on from the other side of the house, and from the dark I could see a woman swing open the door. She was a good forty feet away, but I could see her walk in, not cautious or scared but like she owned the place. She came to the middle of the room and opened the double glass doors to the front balcony and stepped out like she was enjoying the view of the lake down below. She came back in and walked in my direction, glancing around, picking up bits of stuff. She finally parked at the table where the phone sat. She thumbed through a note pad and punched the answering machine and listened to Lester calling Callie all whiney from the Sierra Peaks the night before. The woman cocked her head like she was trying to remember something and played the message again from the top so she could hear Callie's voice on the greeting. She didn't hear me slip into the kitchen and stop about eight feet from her.

"Help you with something?"

She turned around cool as can be but didn't get up.

"I didn't think anyone was here," she said.

"That's kind of obvious."

She stood up and stuck out her hand. She wasn't much older than me and wore high-end hiking clothes. "I'm Nora Ross. I'm an attorney."

"The L.A. lawyer who called Callie yesterday. Heard your message."

"Is Ms. Dean home?" she asked. She smiled a real pretty smile "She's expecting me." When I didn't answer right off, she lost the smile.

"She has made some troubling demands on my office," she said, hard as nails. "I suggest she see me without delay."

"Callie's dead. Died last night about two hours after you talked to her."

If she was shocked, she didn't let on. "What happened?"

"Car wreck. Went off the road when she was on her way to meet your Jerry Q. about half an hour north of here."

"That's awful," she said. "But he's not my Gerald Q."

"You're the lawyer for the missing guy's wife, right?"

"My firm is her attorney of record," she said. "I'm just an associate." She sat back down. "I have a condo down in Mammoth, so the firm thought I was the obvious choice to come up here because I know the country."

She kind of looked me up and down then—the packer boots, the knife and stone on the belt of the Wranglers, the shirt with the horseshoe-nail tears at the cuffs, the neck rag, the sunburn, the puffy eyes from no sleep, the skinned knuckles, and the big hat, and maybe figured she didn't know the same country I did. I hung my hat on a chair.

"Anyway," she said, "the firm felt I could at least find due north on a map."

"Fair enough."

"The crash," she said. "It was an accident, right?"

"Don't think so. She was heading to meet this clown up at State Line. She left us a note about it right over there on the refrigerator, but somebody's lifted it. Then less than twenty four-hours later an old packer named Albert Coffey gets burned to death at State Line supposedly cooking some meth."

She gave me a so-what sort of shrug.

"Albert's drug of choice was a pint of Jim Beam and a sixpack. But the billionaire's boy knew who this stove-up drunk was. Gerald e-mailed the county sheriff that Albert claimed to have seen a dead man alive last winter."

"Did he?" she asked. She didn't sound happy about that notion.

"Nope."

Now the girl looked as confused as hell. "You have two suspicious deaths a day apart? What do the authorities say?"

"Nothing. Just two real sad accidents. Twenty miles apart, but two different county jurisdictions in two different states. Be dog years before anybody makes a connection except for Sarah Cathcart. She's a deputy here and already smells something rank."

"I've spoken to her on the phone," she said, "and she told me she knows absolutely nothing of a wrecked plane."

The woman opened a bag and pulled out a notebook and pawed through it. "You must be either Thomas Smith or Lester Wendover."

"I'm Smith."

"Alright," she said, looking me over again like she was trying to square me with whatever she had in the notebook, "you're saying Callie Dean told the truth about the plane?"

"Oh yeah."

"She saw it?"

"Nope. Lester and me found it way in the back country three days ago."

"But you didn't notify the authorities."

I opened the fridge. "Beer?"

"Oh, that would be great," she said. She got a sour look when she saw it was only Corona, but I opened it and she took it.

"Old Callie wanted to contact the family first. Every last one of them."

"So she contacted Gerald as well as my firm?"

"Lester did. Kinda by mistake, but he talked to him alright."

"And now," she said, "you think Gerald was responsible for Callie Dean's death."

"I think he flat had her killed. Then Albert Coffey too."

She diddled with her pen on the table. "How?" she asked.

"Don't know exactly. It looks like he's got some Cubans working for him up here. At least two guys and maybe a girl. And they're just the ones I've seen."

"And you know for sure he's in this area?" she said.

"He's here. Saw him not more than an hour and a half ago up at State Line. Recognized him from the Internet."

That got her.

"And he knew me, too. Sonofabitch waved at me."

"Then you know something about him," she said. "About his arrest when he was in college for flying in marijuana from the Caribbean. About his connection to Cuban exile traffickers?"

"Some. I know he and the stepmom are duking it out over the estate."

"Respectable people commit murder for piddley little life insurance policies," she said. "We're talking hundreds of times that on the line."

I drank my beer.

"Gerald is a huge disappointment to his father," she said. "For years since his arrest he's refused to use his family name, just the middle initial, the GQ gangsta nonsense. His rebuke to his dad. And he lapses into this phony Latin thing. Very Scarface. Very un-PC."

"Imagine your disappointment."

She gave me a funny look like she was seeing me for the first time.

"Years ago," she said, "his mother, the first wife, had his father set up a trust for him. A really hefty allowance, but he couldn't get his hands on the principal until he's forty—in about a year and a half."

"A lot?"

"A percentage of the estate," she said. "High eight figures. Low nine."

"Pretty soon you'll be talking real money."

She sort of smirked. "Now Gerald's stepmother has possession of a revised trust which revokes the bequest should the father die for any reason." She started rooting through her bag again. I thought she just happened to have that very same trust in there and was about to whip it out. Instead, she pulled out a big old wrapped Subway.

"When Gerald was really coked-up about a year ago," she said, "he told his dad the old man was worth more to him dead than alive. With GQ's drug connections, his father took it as a tangible threat. For now, any bequest is totally at the father's discretion." She held up the sandwich. "Would you like some of this? I'm absolutely famished."

She didn't look famished. When I nodded yeah she got up, and I watched her from the back getting plates and napkins from the kitchen like the cabin was hers. Her legs were firm and smooth-muscled like she did sports or ran.

"Silver's in the left drawer."

"Thanks," she said. She turned around and caught me looking. "Our client is considerably younger than her husband. She's closer to Gerald's age, and quite attractive."

It was a monster sandwich with lots of turkey and cheese and tomatoes and peppers. She cut it in half with the paper still on, then put out the plates with stale Doritos from the cabinet. She parked herself at the table, and we started to eat.

"Anyway," she said, "when our client gets her husband declared legally dead, which is only a matter of time, Gerald loses hugely."

"So the clock's wound for old GQ too."

"Most definitely," she said. "His father gave him a time frame to clean up his act."

"Giving the spoiled bastard one last chance to man-up?"

"Well put," she said. "But if he's dead, Gerald's toast."

She went back to her half of the sandwich. Girl had herself an appetite. After a bit she stopped for breath, daubed her mouth, and sipped her beer.

"Our investigators feel that he's into the Cubans for staggering amounts. So it's not just that he places his helicopters at their disposal or launders their money. With his allowance he's became another cash cow. They'll push his interests to protect their own. But without the promise of a huge payday," she wobbled her hand back-and-forth, "I wouldn't want to be Gerald if Dad is legally deceased. So now he maintains that his father is alive, hiding out in some place like Cabo. Sipping 'ritas with senoritas to escape his ball-busting second wife." She stopped and wiped her mouth again. "I should shut up. I'm being indiscreet."

"You know he's going to report the wreck himself and make chumps out of you folks."

She didn't like that. "I know he's planted the seed of doubt in the probate judge's mind that there is a possibility his father's alive," she said. "You can see how our client finds this all very frustrating."

"Just imagine how Callie and Albert feel."

"I'm sorry," she said. Then she straightened up all of a sudden and smiled. "But Gerald won't report the wreck. If he does, his father's body gets ID-ed. Game over."

"He took the body."

"Shit."

I told her about the tampered wreck, the cleaned-up cockpit, the fake note with the bogus story that the dead guy had walked out safe, and how that tied in with the bullshit that Albert had given the guy a lift eight months ago. I told her about the meth planted in Callie's car and how I figured there'd probably be some little trace of the dead guy planted in Albert's Firebird too.

"Terrific," she said. "All Gerald has to do now is show somebody the wreck."

"Trap's been set."

"But Gerald's father is dead," she said. "You saw the body?"

"He's dead, alright. Lester and me were as close to the body as I am to you."

"That, Sergeant Smith," she said, "makes you both very inconvenient people to leave walking around."

I must have tensed up when she called me that.

"GQ's not the only one who does his homework," she said. "How long were you over there?"

"Two tours."

"I can't imagine that," she said.

There wasn't much to say to that.

"Can I ask you something?"

I shrugged okay.

"You're obviously a smart and competent guy. Despite the artful lack of grammar. Callie Dean has been stirring the pot on this with our client in a way that borders on extortion. Why didn't you just report the wreck three days ago before your friends started complicating things?"

I told her about Lester stealing the watch and the money. About not wanting folks to brand Lester as some thief.

"I was just trying to keep Lester's dick out of the ringer. Mine too, I guess. I should've known you can't lie your way to the truth."

"You're obviously not a lawyer," she said.

Chapter Nine

I got us another couple of Coronas, and she talked and talked like we were old gossip pals. About Gerald concocting what she called a false narrative out of little bits of fact. Stuff that you could add up and say there's reasonable doubt the guy's not dead. She was still talking when I saw headlights arcing through the trees, then die just as quick.

She watched me dump our plates and bottles in the trash, snag my hat, and open the side door to the deck. When she started to say something, I grabbed her bag and handed it to her. Then I grabbed her arm hard and put my finger against my lips and shook my head. I led her out to the deck and stopped. We could hear a car motor humming on the other side of the house. When that stopped, there was just the sound of the breeze in the aspen until the click of car doors opening and that hollow clack the snapping-in of a magazine on an AK-47 makes. The drive curved up behind the house almost as high as the eaves, so Nora's car was parked just above us, blocking their way. She glanced at her car, then at me, and nodded like we should make a run for it. I shook my head no and led her as quiet as I could across the deck to four wooden steps that led down into the trees. We were in plain sight of anybody standing near her car.

The Cubans didn't worry about noise. They thumped down the stairway on the other side of the house and pushed in the same door Nora had used. They flipped on the lights and deployed fast. Through the windows I could see there were three of them, the two from the Sierra Peaks and a third who seemed to be in charge. That guy was huge. All three carried weapons. We eased down the steps, and I turned back to look. Their car was one of those big Escalades, black naturally, and most likely a rental. When we got to the dirt, we made a racket in dead leaves and twigs, but nothing like the racket coming from the house. I heard stuff break and furniture skid and a splintering sound like a door got kicked off the frame. I still had hold of Nora's arm. I nodded downhill. We slipped around to the front of the deck in a crouch and headed back toward the house. The part of the deck in the front of the house facing the lake made a narrow sort of balcony. I led Nora under it. Rolls of tarpaper and old five-gallon plastic paint cans were piled near the concrete foundation with a long section of half-rolled chicken wire. There were two paper sacks of cement that had got wet and set hard. I made a nest in the tarpaper, then a little barrier of the loose wire with the cement sacks anchoring it for weight, and we scrunched down in the dirt with the balcony planks about six feet over our heads, careful not to actually touch the wire and set it jiggling. Light poured down from the main room through the spaces between the boards, and they could have seen us if they'd thought to look. I took my knife from my belt and opened the blade and set it just next to my hand. I sifted some dirt on it so it wouldn't catch the light. Somebody swung open the glass doors to the deck and stepped out. The boards creaked overhead, and we could see bits of moving shadow. Then I heard the quick double-click of somebody racking the slide of an automatic, maybe a Sig-Sauer like the Navy SEALS use, but I couldn't be sure.

"Your car is here, lady," the guy said, semi-loud. "We know you're here too. Come on out—*por favor*. We'll make friends. I'll make you soup."

We heard the other two idiots laughing from inside. There was a clattering of something dumped on the boards like plastic. A couple of little white pieces fell over the balcony onto the dirt just downhill. A couple of plastic soda bottles thumped down too. I could hear Nora starting to breathe real loud, panicking. I slipped an arm around her and pulled her in. A second pair of footsteps trotted across the boards, and I heard a different voice talking Spanish. The first voice, the huge guy, said something. His big creaky footsteps went back into the house. The lighter footsteps moved and creaked from directly overhead to the deck we'd just crossed, moving away from us, but closer to the four steps we'd just used. I listened to hear if the guy was coming down into the trees, and moved a bit so I could see if he was heading back around our way. For a second all I could hear was Nora breathing, softer now. There was a big old ringing clank of something metal hitting the propane tank above the drive, and a car door closing. Either there were more of them or someone was checking out Nora's car, probably getting the VIN off the doorjamb.

Nora started to tremble and I pulled her close, her back to my front while I watched the corner of the foundation for anyone coming. She was sweating from fear, and it made her perfume strong. Probably strong enough to smell from half a dozen feet away. I tapped her on the jaw with my finger so she'd turn her head and look back at me. I put my finger to my mouth again and pointed to myself, the dirt, then back to her. Then I moved my flattened palm down in a stay-put, be-cool motion and she nodded.

I kept my eyes on the corner of the foundation while I scooped handful after handful of damp earth and rotting leaves that had blown under the balcony and sprinkled them over us both, starting with our feet, which I halfway buried, then our legs and the rest, all the way to our heads. Since her legs were bare, I wanted to take the sweat sheen off them that a flashlight could pick up. Pretty soon instead of that nice girly, citrusy smell, she had the old dead-leaf and damp earth smell you get under a house. I stretched behind me for what handfuls of leaves and twigs I could reach and sprinkled them over us till we were both covered like crumb donuts. When I saw the flashlight beam, I stopped. I wrapped that arm around Nora real slow and let my other hand rest on the knife. We could hear footsteps crunching in the leaves and dirt coming our way. Then I said the only thing to her I remember saying.

"Don't open your eyes."

She nodded the littlest bit, then was still. She got with the program real quick. I could barely feel her breathe. I kept my eyes closed enough so a flashlight wouldn't pick up the whites, but I could see the light rake over us and the wire and the rolls of tarpaper. The light stopped and moved on. I could feel the unrolled chickenwire quiver when he bumped it with his foot, and I could hear the guy breathe and smell the nightclub stink of cologne and sweat. We were in plain sight for the guy to see, but I was hoping the wire would work like a camo net and make his eyes focus just enough on it so he wouldn't notice us through the mesh. I didn't think I could get upright and at him with the knife in time if he did.

After a minute he kept on walking, making a circle around the house. We could hear him huffing as he climbed the deck on the far side of the house where they'd come in. Then I could feel Nora take some deep breaths and squeeze my arms, her whole backside pushing against me. I squeezed back.

We lay there listening to doors slamming and window sashes banging shut. I jumped up and pulled her on her feet. They were making so much noise above, I figured I could whisper.

"We gotta get away from the house."

I took her hand and we snuck back the way we came, walking slow at first, heading parallel to the paved road down below. When we crossed the dirt drive we broke into a trot into the trees. After a minute we stopped for breath, then with me still grabbing her hand we climbed the face of the hill until we were looking down on the roof of the cabin about fifty yards behind us. The aspens were thick, and I found us a good spot behind some deadfall. The Cubans had left all the lights on, so we could see them clear. The three came together on the drive between Nora's Infiniti and the Escalade. There was talking and pointing. One of them checked the propane tank, and the big one started the SUV. The third guy argued with the big guy, then tiptoed down the steps real careful until he disappeared behind the house. We hunkered when the headlights blazed on, but there was no way they could see us, as high up as we were. The Escalade backed down the drive all the way to the pavement. They were out of sight, but we could see by the headlights that they were turning around. There was a whoosh and a poof and the sound of all the windows breaking out at once as the gas exploded. We could see the fire all orange inside the cabin. It didn't take long.

"My car," Nora said.

We watched for a minute. I grabbed her hand again, and we headed out fast over uneven ground and fallen logs and saplings toward where I'd left the pickup, careful to keep far enough away from the road and out of sight if the Escalade drove by.

That didn't take long either. The Cubans drove up along the lake toward the campgrounds, rolling slow, raking the trees on one side and the water on the other side with their big flashlights. All we had to do was stand still.

"Are we okay?" she asked.

"As long as they don't spot my truck."

It was only a minute or two before the Escalade cruised back faster now, heading toward Piute Meadows.

We walked downslope through tangled aspen saplings till we spotted the Dodge. I felt her watching me getting madder and madder fighting the branches, but keeping her mouth shut until we got to the truck. She asked me for a rag or a towel and if it would be safe to cross the road to the lake and wash. We both looked like we'd taken a roll with the hogs. I rooted around behind the seat and grabbed a flannel shirt. I pulled out my .270, cussing to myself.

"Why didn't we just come here first?" she asked.

"If they'd seen the truck we'd have been goners. Besides, I needed to know what they were doing."

"Then why are you so mad? My god, we're alive."

"I left this." I held up the .270. "I must be getting stupid."

"Would it have made a difference?"

"It would've to them three."

She made a face, but I wasn't really watching. I took her hand and walked her across the road and down some rocks and boulders to the water. We were around a curve, so we couldn't see what was left of the cabin but we could see flame reflecting all across the lake. If headlights came by we could duck down easy enough. I sort of hoped they'd come back.

She unlaced her boots and tried to shake the dirt out of her shirt, then just said the hell with it and stripped down to her underwear and waded out thigh deep. She tensed in the cold water, but she didn't complain.

"You want me to turn around?"

"If you have to ask, it probably doesn't matter," she said. She shivered. "I've had boyfriends I haven't been as close to as we just were under that house."

She almost fell face down in the water at the boom of the propane tank blowing. That was loud enough to hear up at the campgrounds. It echoed in that mountain pocket hard enough we felt the shock wave before we saw the flame shoot up above the treetops lighting up the sky.

"Oh my god" was all she said.

She finished washing up in a hurry then. She pulled her bra away from her and shook out the dirt. Her underwear was indoor stuff, not outdoor. I set the rifle upright in the rocks and went as far as taking off my shirt and neck rag and shaking them out, and rinsing my face and hair and neck as fast as I could with that icy water. I kept my eye on the fire. The whole hillside was lit up like a torch. When she was done I helped her out of the lake and over the rocks. She was shivering more, and I wrapped her in the old shirt and rubbed her down.

"You scared me when you pulled out the knife," she said.

"Probably not much I could have done."

She sort of leaned in to me and her heat just poured out. I held the shirt tight around her. "I doubt that," she said. "It was like you were on a mission or something."

"Was that your car or a rental?"

"Mine," she said.

I let go of her and handed her her own shirt. She shook it out again and put it on.

"What were all those white plastic things they were scattering around?" she asked.

"I don't know. Probably inhalers, cold medicine, that sort of junk. They most likely had solvents and stuff in the soda bottles they tossed around so it'd look like Callie and her pals were running some sort of meth lab in the kitchen."

"Her pals," Nora said, "being you and Lester Wendover."

"That'd be about right."

"You can turn around for a second," she said. But she was halfway out of her wet underpants before I got turned. She shinnied into her shorts and sat on a rock to pull on her hiking boots.

"You knew they were going to blow up the house," she said.

"When I heard them closing all the doors and windows, yeah. I figured they'd be dousing the pilots and turning on the gas so it'd be just another accident, like oh gee that stupid Callie Dean and her pals left the stove on. No crime, just a dumb tweaker getting careless."

She started rooting in her bag and pulled out a big cell phone. "Shouldn't we call the fire department?"

"It'd be the Forest Service, and somebody most likely has. You probably won't get service with that anyway."

"It's a satellite phone," she said.

"Then I'll be borrowing it."

"So what did you learn under the house that was worth almost getting us both killed?" She said it with a smart-girl look, like she figured not a damn thing.

"Well, now I know you'll never find the old man's body."

"Why?"

"They most likely dissolved it in a barrel of lye like the Mexican cartel guys do to each other. The fella who does it they call *El Pozolero*."

"What's that?"

"The soupmaker."

She made a grossed-out face.

"Now we got to figure what to do with you tonight."

"What do you want to do with me tonight?"

When I didn't answer, she almost laughed. "I don't suppose they have car rentals here in town?"

"Get real."

"Then I'm stranded," she said.

"If you got friends down in Mammoth, have them come get you. Was your car registered there or L.A.?"

"Santa Monica," she said.

"Then you'll be safe in Mammoth."

"I have a condo for skiing," she said. "I don't know a soul in town."

"Then you need to get your butt back to that office on Wilshire Boulevard. Once they run your registration, they'll know the widow's troops are all over this county, same as them. They'll know they got to pick up the pace."

She took my hand again and we climbed up the rocks to the road. You could almost feel the heat from the fire, but she was shaking. When we got back to the truck I set the .270 upright between us and asked her for her phone. She handed it over and showed me how to work it. First I called Power Line Creek. May answered. She was crying. She said Mitch had just left after telling her and Harvey that Albert was dead. She said that Harv had driven out to the Bonner and Tyree ranch to tell Dan Tyree, whose dad had been Albert's cousin and gone with him to Vietnam and didn't come back. She figured Harvey had gone in person because

Dan's mom would be sure to pour him a stiff one. Then she apologized for blubbering and said she was okay and that Albert was at peace now, free of his demons. Lester was there, and he'd sit with her till Harvey got home. I told her to hang on to Lester and not let him leave until I picked him up tomorrow. Then I dialed Dave Cathcart's to see if Sarah was home, but I punched the off button before it rang and just handed the phone back to Nora.

Chapter Ten

"So what *are* you going to do with me tonight?" she asked. We were in my pickup creeping along the lake road toward the burning house. We could see the Forest Service fire trucks zipping our direction with lights flashing at the far end of the lake.

"Stash you in a motel in town under my name. In the morning you can call a rental car company in Reno and have them drive something down for you if you want to stick around."

"Will they do that?" she asked.

"What else they got to do?"

"Will you go back to your pack place?" she asked.

"Not till morning. There's probably somebody watching the logging road. It'll be safer by daylight. I'll catch some winks parked in some ranch lane somewheres."

When we got opposite the house, it was falling in on itself and the fire was burning uphill away from the lake.

The Forest Service crew would have themselves a hike. There was a smudge of black smoke from the Infiniti that stood out from the orange flames and white smoke against the night sky. I looked over and Nora was just staring.

"That could have been us," she said.

Now she had time to think about being scared all over again. She started shaking like she was going to puke.

"Hey. You did good back there. I had guys on patrol weren't as calm as you."

"But you weren't scared," she said.

"I was so scared I would've pissed my britches, but I didn't want to embarrass myself in front of a pretty girl. That's why I squeezed you so tight."

She knew I was bullshitting, but it loosened her up.

"I thought that was some primitive cowboy courting ritual," she said.

"Up here everything is a primitive cowboy courting ritual."

It was too bad about the cabin. I told her about the buffalo over the fireplace and that I was sorry he'd be joining his ancestors in the great beyond. I liked that buffalo even if he didn't belong in this country. I said that burning him would be bad medicine for the Cubans. She just looked at me like I was nuts.

When the Forest Service got close, I stopped the Dodge in my lane until they shot by me, two pumpers and a crew truck. There was no place to pull over without landing in the lake. They'd need more help before the night was over.

"So this," she looked at the mountain on fire, "this still won't be on anyone's radar."

"Nope. Just another meth fire fifty miles from Albert's. Just another sorry accident. But when Gerald's guys find me, they'll have to shoot me and Lester too. That won't look like an accident, so they'll probably shoot one of their own and leave the surprised sonofabitch with some cash lying next to us so it'll look like a meth deal gone bad. Frémont county will have this little mini shit-kicker crime wave, and that'll be that."

"Deranged veteran dies in drug double cross," she said.

"That's me. Then Gerald will call in the wreck a couple of days later and folks will get distracted and forget all about us."

"We shouldn't get killed over this," she said. "It's not in an associate's job description."

"What the hell is an associate, anyway?"

"An errand-girl with a quarter-million dollar education."

I just kept driving.

"So. What if when GQ calls that wreck in, it ain't there?"

She gave me a funny look. "I don't get it."

"If there's no wreck, it's old Gerald who gets put in the middle of a lie. A big-time hoax on cable news. The county'll send in a chopper and there'd just be a bare hunk of mountain. The law will start asking him questions he can't answer, and Nancy Grace and Anderson Cooper will be on his ass. Once folks call you a liar nowadays, you're branded a liar for good."

"That would be brilliant," she said. "But how do you make an entire airplane disappear?"

"Hadn't got that far."

"I thought you said you can't lie yourself to the truth," she said.

"I'm way past the truth."

We didn't talk much the rest of the way in to town. I cruised side streets looking for Cubans and Escalades and finally dropped her off in front of the county sheriff's. I parked in the lot behind the bank and walked the dirt alley to the back side of the Ponderosa Motel, watching the shadows. I left the .270 in the truck. Carrying it into the motel office would be a little too Western, even for Piute Meadows. I rented a motel room from a woman clerk I didn't know and said it was for my girl cousin from Winnemucca. When I got back, Nora Ross was sitting on the curb outside the sheriff's station like a dirty teenage runaway, not some hot L.A. lawyer. If any deputy walked out and saw her, I don't know what she would have said. I picked up her bag and led her down the back alley to the Ponderosa parking lot. We didn't see a soul on our way to the room. I unlocked it, handed her the key, then did a quick look-through of the closet and bathroom. The walls were painted-over cinderblock and would slow down a high-velocity round if it came to that. She wanted me to stand guard while she showered off, so while I waited I turned off the lights and watched the street. I heard her open the bathroom door and felt her walk up warm and steamy behind me and felt her finger run along my back.

"I don't want to be alone here tonight," she said.

I watched the street for another minute. It was bright under the arc lights and quiet as a tomb.

"I'll just get my rifle."

I drove her down to Mammoth before sunup so she could get clean clothes and rent a car. Just a quick hundred mile round trip over two eight-thousand-foot passes. We put twenty-five miles behind us before we stopped for breakfast in the little town at the foot of the Tioga road. She ate like a trucker and asked me more about making the plane disappear. Then she said she was afraid she was going to die there under the house the night before. She had only heard about such people and always figured that her family and her job and her education made her safe from that part of the world. I started to say something lame but pretty much just let her talk.

We went outside and walked toward the truck. The town was on the high side of the basin, and she was admiring the big blue prehistoric lake off in the distance. Up close it was all salt grass, alkali mud, and swarms of flies. In the bright sun we just blended in with the tourists stopping off on their way to Yosemite.

We were kind of quiet for a while. She'd been pretty sweet the night before, but scared. When she woke up at three a.m. and found me standing at the window in the dark, she'd got out of bed and without saying anything we watched the street together, empty except for a big rig every now and then, or some fisherman just pulling into town after driving half the night up from L.A., her leaning back smooth against me and me just holding her with the Remington in easy reach.

"You look sad," she'd said.

"My dad always said if you lived right and told the truth, you could look any man in the eye and tell them to go to hell."

"Can't you do that now?"

"No ma'am. I sure couldn't."

"I'm not your mother," she said. She took my hand and led me back to the bed. "Don't call me ma'am."

I followed her. I guessed all the Cubans and acid cooks were all tucked in for the night.

We were coming off Deadman Summit fifteen minutes outside Mammoth when she started to kind of laugh to herself.

"Moving the plane would be a fantastic trick if it wasn't so absolutely illegal." She looked happy, like the lawyer brain was working overtime.

I dropped her off at her condo. It was just wood and glass like eight thousand others on the way to the chair lifts, which always looked ugly once the snow melted. She gave me her satellite phone number and an awkward sort of kiss, and said she'd track me down that afternoon. When I drove back out to the Reno Highway, I saw she'd left a balled up wad of something purple on the seat. It was her damp underpants she'd taken off at the lake. I hung them on the rearview mirror like I was in high school and headed back north. It was only about eight in the morning.

I picked up Lester at Power Line Creek. Harvey was gone to Frémont Lake Reservation to talk to Albert's relatives, so I didn't tell May about seeing the cabin burning the night before, only about being up at State Line.

"I always knew that Callie Dean was bad news," she said when Lester was outside. "But I never thought Albert was into that junk."

She noticed my filthy clothes but didn't say anything.

I could tell she was trying not to cry. I gave her a hug, grabbed Lester, and got the hell out of there. Lester looked like crap too, but he was doing his best to maintain. Once we were in the truck I told him about the cabin. And I told him that GQ wasn't his pal anymore. He got pretty depressed about Callie's stuff burning up so he wouldn't have as much to remember her by. He made a crack when I pulled the panties off the mirror and stuffed them in my glove box, but his heart wasn't in it. He never asked whose they were.

I hit the bridge below town too fast with my eyes on the Ponderosa Motel and was in the 25 MPH zone before I knew it. When I looked sideways to check out the Highway Patrol office, Lester hollered to slow down. Up ahead Albert's Firebird was dangling behind a tow truck right in the middle of the street. I pulled over just past the tow truck. Sarah was standing in front of the Dunbar garage talking to a tall guy in a Hawaiian shirt and mesh cowboy hat. Before I got out I wagged my finger at Lester.

"Just once in your life, do exactly what I say like your damn life depends on it, which it probably does."

"What're you talking about?" he said.

"Just stay in the damn truck."

"Jesus, relax," he said. "But don't take all day."

I got out, and they watched me walk up like they'd been talking about me.

"Hey, Tommy," Sarah said. "How's Dad's colt?"

"Settling in."

"Did you hear about the fire at the lake last night?"

"I was there."

The man looked up then but didn't say a word. Sarah reached out to brush some dirt from the night before off my sleeve. The dirt didn't come off.

"I called the owner down in Palo Alto," Sarah said. "Told her it looked like a chemical or gas fire. The Forest Service found Pepsi bottles full of solvent like you use for making meth along the drive and pseudoephedrine pills scattered everywhere. She was pretty steamed."

"Hard to blame Callie when she's dead."

"Yeah," Sarah said. "But it was a Forest Service lease. They probably won't let her rebuild."

"That sucks."

"Meth," the guy said. He smiled like his spaceship had just landed. "Hillbilly heroin."

"This is Jerry from Florida," Sarah said. "Or I should say Gerald. It was his father who disappeared last winter."

"Yeah, I know. The famous GQ."

He didn't stick out his hand and neither did I. He wore a big gold watch. It looked just like the one that Lester stole. I pointed at the car on the hoist.

"If you're strapped for cash, you can probably pick up this Firebird cheap."

"Someone named Albert Coffey left a message with my dispatcher last winter about seeing my dad," he said. "I just found out about it. That's why I'm up here. Boy am I sorry he died before I got a chance to ask him about it."

"Hey, you missed him by a whisker, bud."

"When he heard about Albert's accident," Sarah said, "Gerald recognized the name and called our office to see if anything of his father's turned up." She held up a clear plastic evidence bag with a blue windbreaker inside. "We just pulled this out of the trunk."

He looked at me real smirky. "Pretty amazing, huh, guy?"

"This is Tommy Smith," Sarah said.

He made a salute with one finger to his hatbrim. "I know all about him," he said. "Bronze Star. Purple Heart. You're quite a man, man."

Sarah tensed up, but she didn't say anything.

"Deputy Cathcart said you worked with Albert Coffey," he said. "That's why I wanted to talk to you. But you and your friend are hard guys to track down out here in open country with dirt roads and no phones."

"Oh, I ain't hard to find."

"No," he said, "now that I know where you live I ought to be able to find you real easy."

"Albert never said shit about missing airplanes, though."

"But he was a drunk, right?" he said. "My dad must have left his jacket in his car, and the guy forgot all about it."

"Yeah. I can see how your old man would've had trouble remembering much himself."

"Maybe he survived the crash then walked away from it," Sarah said. "With memory loss or something."

"Wouldn't be the first crash the old scamp walked away from," he said. "But now we got real proof he survived." He looked happy as could be. "That he's, you know, out there somewhere."

"Hey, maybe he was up at State Line with you yesterday, smoking crank with Albert Coffey."

"Tommy!"

"Tommy," he said, mimicking that tone she gets.

"Albert was no tweaker. And neither was Callie Dean."

"Well," GQ said with that sour-lemon smirk, "folks don't need to do drugs to make money off scum who do." He looked Sarah up and down. "I bet you see a lot of meth up here, right, Deputy Sarah?"

"Hardly any right here, actually," she said. She usually didn't like it when guys checked her out like that. "We've been lucky, right, Tommy?"

"Up here, meth is as rare as Cubans."

He gave us another stoner smile and lit a smoke.

"So, Gerald, how come your old man would hide out? Walk away from all his cash?"

He puckered his mouth around that cigarette and fiddled with the fake stampede string under his chin.

That hat irritated the hell out of me. "Could be he just wanted to start a new life. His wife is a ball-breaking whore, excuse my French, Sarah. Who knows what wild hair guys that age get? Dad had a friend from Silicon Valley worth millions and millions. He gets in his sloop a while back, sails out the Golden Gate toward the Farallones in the fog to scatter his mother's ashes—touching, no?—and just disappears. Poof. Sinks without a trace. They don't find so much as a life jacket. Nada. So now his friends are thinking he staged a disappearance. Like Dad."

"Damn. An epidemic of rich pricks who're tired of all their money. Makes about as much sense as a meth epidemic in Piute Meadows."

"Maybe it was post traumatic stress like you soldiers get," he said. "What did *you* do in Iraq, sergeant?"

"Did my best to keep my boys safe."

"Wow," he said, insulting as hell. "What did you have to do to do that?"

"Kill whoever wanted us dead."

"Did they give you your medal for that?" he asked.

"We're all real proud of Tommy," Sarah said. "And we're just glad he's home in one piece."

"Then you should try to stay in one piece," he said.

Sarah was about to say something when Lester stumbled out of the truck.

"This the rich choad from Florida?" he asked.

"This gentleman thinks we have evidence about his father's disappearance," Sarah said.

Gerald smiled at Lester. "*Por fin,*" he said, "*la verdad.*"

Lester looked GQ over. GQ quit smirking. He was taller than Lester, but even as beat up as Lester was right then, he was in real good shape and flat fearless in a fist-fight. GQ sensed that right off.

"You got some unfinished business with Callie Dean," Lester said. "You'll be finishing it with me."

Gerald flicked his cigarette into the street. Then he stepped off the curb out of reach and kind of hunched his shoulders and wiggled his fingers at Lester like some old-movie witch doctor and made a spooky-lookey sort of moan. He trotted across the street laughing like a moron.

I put my hand on Lester's chest. "Easy, bud."

"Don't forget what I said, deputy," GQ hollered back.

Sarah just watched him go. "He'd be a pretty good-looking guy," she said, "if he didn't slump so much."

Lester looked at her like he couldn't tell if she was kidding or not. "I'm going to get a ham-and-cheese and a beer," he said. "You guys want something?"

"We're good," Sarah said quick, like she wanted him to just go.

We watched Lester walk down the sidewalk to the bakery. Across the street GQ opened the door of a white Mercedes with Nevada plates and took out a little man-purse. He took off his hat and left it on the seat, then he walked to the front of the Mansion House hotel. There was a new Range Rover with California plates parked just behind the Mercedes. Three guys waited for him on the sidewalk, not Cubans but rich-looking old white guys. GQ handed the car keys to one of them, and they went inside the hotel. Sarah just stared like she was sorting it all out.

"So what the heck was that all about?" Sarah asked.

"He was the one had Callie run off the road."

"I guessed that much," she said. She reached into her shirt pocket and pulled out a piece of paper and handed it to me. It was Callie's note to Lester and me about driving to meet GQ at State Line. "I wasn't born yesterday."

"Weren't saying you were." I folded the note and handed it back. I looked across the street. We could see GQ and his pals sitting at a window table in the dining room looking at menus. "Who the hell are those guys?"

"Friends of Gerald's father from the Flying W aviation club," she said. "One's a big real-estate guy from L.A. They were in the office first thing this morning stinking of money." She got one of her why-do-I-put-up-with-this bureaucratic-crap looks. "Mitch had a meeting of the officers on duty and told us to extend them every courtesy. They said they're starting up the search again, this time further west where nobody looked before."

"Where?"

"Here. This quadrangle."

"When?"

"Couple of days," she said. "Why so interested?"

"Just curious. Maybe they think Albert gave them a new lead."

"I guess so," she said. "Or Callie. Since she's been calling the family's lawyers, they've been calling me. All about that plane. So why was she going to meet him?"

"You read the note. She didn't say."

"But she told you what she was up to," she said.

"Only that she wanted to shake some money from that family. I told her it was a bad idea."

She just stared at me like she didn't much believe me.

"So now old Gerald is surrounded by his own kind, all rich and connected."

"What I don't know is why," she said.

"Money talks."

"More than I can say for you," she said. "Whatever she was up to, you don't need to cover for Callie anymore."

I just nodded.

"I'm cutting you a lot of slack," she said, "in case you haven't noticed."

"I noticed. How come?"

"Because the quieter you get, the more you worry me."

"I just want to backtrack Callie and make sure Lester's out of whatever nonsense she was scheming."

"You'll tell me what you know sooner than later."

"Yes ma'am."

"Stay away from this guy in the meantime. I don't like that he's checked out your record."

"Can I ask you something?"

"Sure," she said. "What?"

"What was it he told you not to forget?"

"I was trying to see if he'd let his guard down," she said. "He started bragging about his expensive toys." She got flummoxed. "Female and otherwise. He said he wanted to see me in a thong on his cigarette boat."

"Hell, Sarah. Isn't a male in this county over twelve wouldn't pay to see that."

"What is that, exactly?" She tried to sound all serious and law-enforcement-y.

"Itty-bitty underpants that run up the crack of your butt, I guess."

She punched me hard on the arm. "A cigarette boat, you jerk."

I rubbed my arm. She was embarrassed as hell.

"You just be careful, Tommy," she said. "I don't know what he thinks you did, but he means you harm."

"I'll sleep with one eye open."

"You never sleep," she said. "That's your problem."

She grabbed my sore arm and marched me across the street and around the corner toward the Mark Twain Café like I was under arrest. We could see GQ and his friends watching us through the window of the hotel. Inside the Mark Twain, we sat down and she bought me my second breakfast that morning. I was wondering how much to tell her, when she had to run off halfway through her Belgian waffle because Lester tracked us down and said that Mitch was looking for her. Fishermen had just found the nude body of some Mexican girl snagged in the willows below the dam.

Chapter Eleven

Lester sat down and watched me eat. He cleaned up Sarah's waffle and went to the can twice in the time it took me to finish. When we got up to leave I thought I saw the black Escalade cruise by, but it disappeared behind the Masonic Lodge before I got a good look. We walked back down Main Street and crossed over to my pickup. The tow truck had hauled the Firebird around the corner out of traffic and left it on the side street where Albert's relatives could pick it up. We stood on the concrete in front of the garage for a bit, Lester talking to old man Dunbar, me just looking at the hotel across the street.

I asked Lester to buy some things we'd need for the Boy Scout trip like nylon stuff sacks, matches, batteries, another box of .270 soft points and such. He didn't see what the hurry was but I made him a list. A week ahead was always pretty abstract for him. We walked past the Sierra Peaks, but he couldn't even look inside so I guessed we'd be taking our dinner trade to the Hunter's Lodge for a while.

Lester kept on toward the sporting goods while I dropped in to the general store to pick up a few camp things that May didn't send up with the groceries like a hard salami, some cheese, Copenhagen that Lester had asked for, half a dozen hacksaw blades, a can of liquid wrench, and a bottle of Crown Royal.

When I stepped out of the store, I saw GQ a block away leaning against my truck. He saw me and started walking my direction. I waited outside the sporting goods by the sidewalk freezer with the trophy-sized Rainbows. When he caught up with me he lit a Camel Filter and smiled at me from behind his shades. He looked like he'd had a pretty good lunch.

"You could use a new truck, cowboy," he said.

"It's paid for."

"You could have a lot nicer one paid for," he said. "You could have a hundred of them, *claro?*" He smoked like a stoner sucking on a joint. We both watched Lester through the window drifting through the stacks of camping and fishing stuff. I didn't want him thinking about a soft target like Lester too much. I walked in the other direction and set my paper bag at the foot of the iron fence by the court-house lawn. He followed right along.

"That's what you want, right," he said, "money?"

"You got no idea what I want."

He made his spooky-lookey noise again, kind of an eeeuuuww sound. I wanted to deck him.

"I figure that's why you and the sidekick haven't told anybody about Dad's plane." He laughed and wagged his finger and sounded real Ricky Ricardo. "You boys are up to something. I can tell."

I just let him talk.

"His girl Callie wanted money," he said. "She sounded like she would've done about anything to get it, too."

"You're lucky Lester don't hear you talking that way. You'd be picking your teeth off the concrete."

"My boy Teófilo was close enough to him last night," he said, "to cut his throat in his sleep."

"So why didn't he?"

"'Cause you're the brains of the outfit, my friend." He reached over and touched the elbow of my dirty shirt just like Sarah had. "I hate to tell you, but your laundry detergent just ain't cutting it."

We both leaned our backs against the fence staring up at the mountains like tourists. I looked down the sidewalk and saw Lester step out of the sporting goods.

"You tell me what works for you," he said. "You can fly with one of the search teams." He damn near giggled. "Be like doing recon back in Iraq for you."

"I didn't do recon."

"We're gonna start in two days," he said. "You and I can get to know each other."

"Way your Cubans are going, you and I'll both be dead in two days." I picked up my grocery bag and followed Lester down the sidewalk to the Dodge. When I got to the truck, I looked back. GQ finally quit staring and pushed himself off the fence and sauntered out into the street.

Lester watched him trot to the opposite sidewalk then head back toward the hotel. He reached into my grocery bag and pulled out the snuff tin.

"What'd the rich boy want?" he asked.

"Nothing."

"You see that watch he had?"

"Yeah. I saw the damn watch, Lester."

I got into the truck, and we drove back to the pack station.

After I'd put on some clean clothes, we dragged a pile of equipment from the tack trailer and laid it out in full outfits on the pack platforms. Sawbucks, saddle pads, cinches and lashropes, panniers or slings, and canvas tarps. I had Lester inventory every piece so we could fix what needed fixing. The platforms were just rough planks out in the sun, so it was hot work shaking out the dust and mouse turds, finding the bags that needed patching and the straps that needed mending. Harvey always bought good equipment, but he had been packing since the world was young, so a lot of his stuff was pretty beat up. Nothing had been touched since last fall, and it didn't look like anything had been mended or oiled since I'd left. Lester cut strips from a piece of latigo-tanned hide for billets and straps, and we punched holes and riveted leather until the sawbucks were all rigged tight as new. I had to pirate a couple of cinches from pack saddles still in the trailer to replace frayed ones so we wouldn't have any sore bellies at ten thousand feet. I made a list for Harvey, so he could order replacement gear.

Somebody had got careless last deer season and left grain in a pretty new bag, and mice had chewed clean through the canvas. I stitched in a latigo patch so the bag would hold a load of bricks.

I kept Lester humming along past noon until we had four full outfits ready to go. Then, Lester being Lester, he was ready to move on to something else.

"I think the rest of this can wait till tomorrow, pard," he said. "Let's grab some lunch and get out of the sun."

We were both sweating, hats on the back of our heads.

"We got other things to do tomorrow, bud."

"What other things?"

"Things."

I rustled us some sandwiches and iced tea, and I kept him at it. An afternoon breeze came up and we got some shade out on the platforms and kept on working until we had six outfits spread out and ready to pack.

Lester stood up and shook himself like a dog. "Should I hang 'em all back inside the shed?"

"No. Let's leave 'em. Just cover each rig with a tarp, then they'll be ready for Harvey to take up to Power Line Creek. That way we won't have to sort 'em twice."

"You know Harv," he said. "He'll just throw 'em in a jumble in the truckbed, and we'll have to root through it next week at four in the damn morning."

He sat on the edge of the platform and ate his sandwich watching the horses in the corral and the sun on the pasture, looking out to the tamarack along the creek with the breeze fluttering the aspen leaves overhead. In the

summer that pack station is about as nice a place as there is
in that country. He watched me snag a halter and walk into
the corral. I slipped a rope over the neck of one of the big
packhorses and checked his new shoes all around. Then I
caught up another and checked him. I could see Lester off
in the shade, taking a pinch of Copenhagen as he wondered
what the hell I was up to. I checked six or eight horses and
mules, then looked over our two best saddle horses and
checked them too. Lester walked up to the fence when I
was picking up the feet of Harvey's big, rangey Quarter
mare that Lester usually rode.

"Figure they'd fallen off in two days?" he said.

"Albert was the one of us who actually liked nailing
on iron."

"We're surely gonna miss old Albert," he said, "in
about six weeks."

"We'll get by."

"Hey," he said, "what did the Florida fruitbat want?
You never said."

I straightened up and let the mare loose. "He wanted
to give us money."

"I knew it," he said. "I *knew* it. Damn, Callie was right."

"He's not giving us squat." I opened the gate, and we
stood there next to Harvey's anvil stump.

"Then why the hell's he offering? Jesus, Tommy, just
admit Callie was right."

"Callie wasn't right. Now because of her this whole
deal is upside down."

"So you're not even going to hear what the man has to
say?" Lester was getting tense.

"I already heard what the man has to say."

"We should go see him," Lester said. "Tonight. Tomorrow at the latest."

"You're going to stay away from that boy, Lester. Like Callie shoulda."

That got him. He was boiling and in my face.

"That guy is our payday." He was yelling now.

"There is no payday. Jesus, Lester, that kind of thinking is what got Callie killed."

He hit me and I went down. He was always quicker than me anyway. I lay back on an elbow and felt around my cheekbone to see if it needed rearranging. My hat was lying in the dirt.

"I don't want to fight you, Lester."

"Then watch what you say, goddamnit," he said. "Watch what you goddamn say." He just stood over me, shouting wild-like, ready to take me out when I got up.

"One more time. No payday. No deal. For ten or twenty mil, you don't think that bastard would cap us on the courthouse lawn in front of the whole town? He killed Callie, bud. Had her run off the road." I rolled over till I could grab the anvil horn and pull myself up. Lester crowded me, ready to swing again. I sat on the anvil. Man, was I clocked. I forgot how hard that boy could hit.

He stood over me still on the fight, snorting through his nose like a horse. "You think dying was her fault."

I didn't answer that.

"Shit," he said. He was thinking about her being lost to him. "Shit." He picked up my hat and threw it at me, then walked off so I couldn't see his face.

I was soreheaded and dizzy the rest of the afternoon. I popped some aspirin and finished up the wiring for the yard lights, splicing in two switches so we could light up the whole canyon if we needed to. Lester wouldn't look at me or talk to me. After about an hour I scribbled down a list and handed it to him. By then he'd quit work altogether and was just sitting on the pack platforms.

"The hell?"

"If you can, gather some of your tools for Harvey. Socket set, screwdrivers, water-pump pliers, and a couple of crescent wrenches. Big ones. Whatever he'll need to pop a head on the GMC. He doesn't have shit for tools up there. Put 'em in a pack box or something so he can pick 'em up next time he's here." If he knew I was lying to him, at least he didn't let on.

I took a break about four and had a beer. Then I haltered up Sarah's dad's colt and led him into the crowding pen by the chute. The pen wasn't as big as I liked, but he wasn't too rank and I could work with him there. I tied a braided cotton rope loose around his neck with a bowline then tied up a hind foot. He fired out and jumped a few times but not so much to make him fall. I started sacking him out easy with a saddle blanket. After about fifteen minutes I left him hobbled and standing quiet to think about things for a time while I gave my head a rest and tended to my rifle. I shook out a pack tarp and spread it down on the platforms and took my scope and a Crown Royal bottle from my saddle pockets and a deerskin bag out of the tin shack, then sat down. I dumped my tools and mounting hardware on the tarp and went to work.

I yanked the bolt and ejected the chambered cartridge, then dropped the floor plate and emptied the magazine and snapped all five rounds into my shirt pocket. Then I set to unscrewing both sights and putting the pieces in a ziplock. I was screwing down the mounting rail when I see this car come down the hill toward the bridge. I pulled one cartridge from my pocket and left that on my lap while I slid the scope onto the rail and kept my eyes on the road. In a couple of minutes a snot-green rental sedan pulled through the aspen with Nora driving and Sarah riding shotgun. I took a sip of Crown Royal and watched them as they piled out and sauntered over. I knew I was in trouble on all sorts of levels. Nora had cleaned up a bunch in the nine hours since I'd left her. Sarah was back in Wranglers and a tank top, her hair stuffed in a ballcap. Nora was talking pretty nonstop.

"Our presumptive widow called Miss Dean back on her cell to give her a piece of her mind," she said. "It never occurred to her that she was leaving her phone number with someone outside her circle who did not wish her well. The very wealthy can be very naïve in their assumptions."

"I guess," Sarah said. "Boy."

"Hi," Nora said when they got close.

"Ladies."

"How's he coming?" Sarah asked. She looked from the colt to the Remington on my lap to the swelling on my cheek. Just like a cop.

"So far so good."

Nora sat next to me.

"Are we going to shoot someone?" she asked.

I just tightened down the mounting rings with an Allen wrench like I did this every afternoon. Nora watched Sarah walk over to the fence by the loading chute.

"Is she going to do something with that horse?"

"No."

"Isn't it her horse?" she asked. "She talked about it in the car." She studied my puffy cheek like she just noticed it.

"Come here," Sarah yelled over. "Show me how he's doing."

It didn't seem like much, but that was about as unlike her as anything I've ever heard Sarah say. I put the tools in the pouch and slid the .270 back in the scabbard and set it on the tarp. I left Nora sitting there and walked over to the fence, snapping the loose round back into my shirt pocket. I untied the hobbles and sacked that old boy out a bit more. I set my saddle on his back easy-like, then took it off and did it again. He quivered the first time the cinch touched his belly, but pretty soon I had it screwed down and was popping the stirrup leathers easy against his sides and rubbing him down with him watching things and figuring it out. He was going to be a nice horse, you could see that right away. Pretty soon Nora followed over.

"Does that hurt him?" she asked.

"No," Sarah said.

I slipped a boot in and stood up in the stirrup for a second, which I normally wouldn't have done for another couple of days if I wasn't showing off like a twelve-year-old. He just stood there, and I eased back down. I unsaddled the colt and loosened the rope, then rubbed him down with just my hand and left him tied while I put my saddle away. Those two followed me to the tack trailer.

"I'd have thought you'd use one of these beat up rigs on him in case he pitched a fit," Sarah said.

"I knew he wouldn't pitch no fit."

That got a funny look from Nora.

"Where's Les?" Sarah asked.

"Hibernating."

The two of them followed me over to the platforms where I'd left my rifle and we all sat.

"This is a beautiful spot," Nora said, but she was glancing around at the storage trailer with the name of a dairy painted on the side but so faded you could barely read it, and the generator parked next to the tin shack, and the housetrailer with the homemade steps. Nora looked like we could have done a lot better by the place. The afternoon breeze was dying off, and it was a real nice time of day. She pointed out to the creek. "Are those ponderosa pines?"

I couldn't tell if she was teasing about the Ponderosa Motel the night before.

"Tamarack."

She kind of wrinkled her face at me.

"Really? I thought tamarack was some sort of larch." She stood up and shaded her eyes. "We had them at summer camp when I was a kid. I remember. Tamarack."

"Where was that?" Sarah asked.

"The Berkshires," Nora said. "Connecticut."

"Out west it refers to a species of lodgepole," Sarah said. "You can call it Sierra Lodgepole or Tamarack Pine. Totally interchangeable."

"I didn't know that," Nora said.

"The proper name is *Pinus contorta*," Sarah said. "They call it that because the subspecies down on the coast are all twisted and gnarly. You know, contorted."

"Like the people, you mean," Nora said.

They were like two old mares switching their tails at each other at feeding time. About then Lester stumbled out of the trailer and sat down on the step. Sarah stood up and ran a finger across the bruise on my cheek.

"Falling out among thieves?" She walked over and sat next to Lester on the trailer steps. Pretty soon they disappeared inside.

"Boy," Nora said. "Cowgirls in tight jeans."

"You don't want to call her that. So what'd you tell her?"

"Nothing," Nora said. "Nothing except what she already knew about Callie Dean's phone calls."

"Are you going to get your tit in a wringer for not coming clean with the law?"

"I beg your pardon?" she asked, but she smiled like I was flirting with her or something. "The firm wants to hold off until they see what move Gerald makes next. Obviously they'd like to catch him coloring outside the lines."

"He'll be doing way more than that. You got your satellite phone on you?"

"It's charging back at the Ponderosa," she said. "The car charger burned up last night."

"I need to borrow it for a couple of days. I'll follow you into town after you leave."

"Can you stay?"

"Nope. Can't risk leaving Lester alone too long."

She just sort of shrugged like she was disappointed. "What are you up to?"

"Better if I don't tell you."

"You're going back up there," she said. "That's why you want my phone." She looked up the canyon. "Is that where it crashed?"

"Yeah. About nine miles back."

Lester and Sarah came down from the trailer with a couple of pitchers and plastic glasses and a big chunk of cheese and set them on the tarp. Sarah poured the three of us all a shot of Crown Royal with ice from the pitcher. She handed a plastic glass to Nora.

"I thought you'd like a whisky with the boys," she said. "Help you settle in to life in the mountains."

Nora looked into her glass at the whisky for a minute, then took a sip and made a face.

"How can you drink this?" she asked. Then she tossed off the rest like a tequila shot and gave a shiver.

Sarah poured herself a big iced tea and sat down next to me on the boards close enough so our shoulders touched.

Lester was eyeing me the whole time to see if I was pissed at him. He downed his drink and poured another shot, then dug his Copenhagen out of his pocket and took a pinch. Nora studied him like he was some Fiji Islander.

"Can I see?" she held out her hand, and he put the snuff tin in it. She opened it and sniffed, making a not-bad face, then handed it back. "We don't see a lot of this on the Third Street Promenade," she said. She looked down at the

Remington laying close enough for her to touch. "Not any of this."

Lester drained his glass then grinned at her over a lip of snuff.

"Alcohol, tobacco, and firearms," he said. "The all-American tri-fecta."

Sarah stood up like she was ready to leave. I remember when I was about fifteen hearing her tell a college girlfriend at the Fourth of July dance that she didn't date local boys because she hated the taste of chew and whisky when she kissed them. That was about all she ever had in common with Callie Dean.

"You want to turn him loose?" I nodded to the colt.

"You should," she said.

"Oh, he won't mind. Your dad picked another good one."

That got a smile out of her, and she almost skipped down to the fence. Inside the pen she talked to the horse a minute before leading him to the pasture gate.

"I didn't tell her about last night," Nora said, "but I think she's figured it out. Women can tell."

"If that old girl knows I slept with you, ain't no way that's good for either one of us."

"That's a double negative," she said.

"Tell me about it."

I headed on down the mountain about twenty minutes after they left and caught up with Nora at the motel. She gave me a little hug once the door was closed. She unplugged the satellite phone charger and handed me the whole rig.

"What do I do now?" she asked.

"You should check out of here and scoot back to Mammoth. Better yet, L.A."

"I should be safe here," she said.

"Well, you're not safe. Not till this thing settles."

"Will you tell me what you're doing?"

"Let's just say I don't plan on waiting around to get shot."

She took a card out of her bag and wrote something on it and stuck it in my shirt pocket.

"That's my cell," she said. "If I wait in Mammoth, will you keep me updated?"

"Yeah."

"I guess I won't feel safe here by myself." She put her arms around me then like she didn't feel safe at all. "Do you ever come to L.A.?"

"Not if I can help it."

I stayed with her longer than I should have. When I left I got her to say she'd check out right after. It was dark when I turned off the Lake Road to the pack station. As I drove through the timber, I could see a glow in the sky from the yard lights before I even got to the drift fence. When I got closer, I saw the glow reflected on the windows of the backpacker cars parked to the side of the aluminum gate. When I turned down the hill toward the creek, the pack station was lit up like a Walmart parking lot. I stopped my truck near the generator and got out, setting the rifle on the hood. I could see Lester inside the trailer eating ice cream by the refrigerator, but with the generator roaring away he never even heard my diesel. Most of the horses were down along the creek, but a few still milled around in the corral. The dust they kicked up swirled in the electric light.

I walked down the road and checked the new switches I'd wired in. When I was done, I went in the trailer.

"Hey."

"Hey," he said, just as loud.

I lit the kerosene lamps.

"I'm going to check the generator. It'll be off for a sec."

He nodded and put away the ice cream. I went back outside and shut it down. The roar faded away, and the yard got black until my eyes adjusted. I walked down the road in the dark and fiddled with a couple more switches, then fired up the generator again, turning on a whole different set of lights. Then I shut it off, picked up my rifle, and went inside. Lester stared at me in the yellow lamplight.

"You might as well put a target on your back, bud."

"I wanted to see what I'm doing," he said.

"You're eating ice cream."

"So?"

"Those bastards are going to take it to us tonight. Maybe tomorrow. No later. They could drive right up to the trailer with Cuban music blasting on their stereo and you couldn't hear them over that noisy sonofabitch."

He watched me set the rifle scabbard on the table.

"So what do we do?"

"You box them tools like I asked?"

"Yeah," he said.

"Then gather your goods for a little pack trip. You and me are heading out by sunup."

"To do what?"

"To get some revenge for Callie Dean."

That made him happy. "Can I take my Ruger?"

"The Ruger would be good."

He started for the back room of the trailer to fetch his gear. For once in his life he wasn't too full of questions. He came back out with a packed stuff-sack.

"So what do we tell Harvey?"

"Nothing. I figure I'll be writing him a check for the use of his animals once he finds out."

"How many?"

"How many pack rigs do we have sitting out there?"

He got it then. "That's gonna cost us plenty, pard."

I started setting out the food we'd take. "Like it hasn't already."

I went outside to snag a set of pack bags. I stopped in the dark outside the tack trailer and studied the trees across the creek and the road where it comes down out of the trees. The moon helped a bit, but it would help someone looking from the other direction just as well. After a minute I went back inside. When we'd packed our goods in the bags and hoisted the bags on the table ready for morning, Lester went off to bed. I pulled the rifle out of the scabbard, got my jacket, and went outside. I thumped the fuel tank on the generator to make sure it was full, and I grabbed the Crown Royal bottle we'd left on the pack platform and walked down the road in the dark.

I found a spot under an aspen in the sagebrush and the rocks above the curve in the road. I was directly facing the bridge. I sat down with Dad's rifle across my lap and waited. The timbered slope facing me was high and kept out a good bit of the moonglow. I was deep in the shadows and pretty much out of sight. I felt wide awake as I watched that bench of the canyon where the logging road cut through like it had for a hundred and fifty years, and I remembered every turn in the road and every big smooth hunk of granite that had been scraped to the side by blade and oxen, and what the washboard road and the creek with the moonlight on it and the bridge would look like through the windshield of a rented Escalade. I sipped the Crown Royal and thumbed the safety off, then pulled it back on again and touched the cartridge box in my jacket pocket and felt for the electrical wire lying next to me in the sagebrush. It didn't seem long until I saw little flickers of light through the black mass of trees down-canyon. After a bit I could see two sets of headlights moving closer up toward the drift fence, then it all went dark. I took another sip of Crown Royal and ran my thumb across the safety again but left it on.

Finally one set of parking lights glowed way up the hill in the clearing by the aluminum gate and started floating down toward me in the dark. The Escalade drifted on down the hill toward the bridge, still with just the parking lights on but outlined by little red and white lights along the running boards and above the tailgate. I couldn't see any sign of the second car. When the Escalade got ten feet from the water, it stopped. One of the Cuban fly fishermen got out of the driver's side and climbed a few feet to stand on the start of that narrow bridge. He was one of the shooters who blew up the cabin and wore a holster on his belt. He took a few steps out on the bridge and looked down at the fast moving creek. He walked back to the car and got in. The electric windows rolled down and the headlights blazed on and hit me right in the face, though I was still more than a hundred fifty feet in front of them. I didn't move, but they wouldn't see me sitting still in the rocks. The driver was watching that bridge.

The Escalade started across, just creeping, correcting a bit from side to side with more room to spare than he thought. When he was almost halfway across, I reached down and felt for the wire and the big plastic switch and thumbed it on. It was a full second before the generator fired up about a hundred yards away and another second until four big halogen spots flared on in a semicircle behind me and lit up that bridge like noon. The Escalade stopped hard, then started to back up, slow at first, the driver half-blind from the spots. I thumbed off the safety then and squeezed off a round into the road on my side of the bridge just so they could hear the shot and see the dirt kick up. The driver hit the gas, and one back wheel started to spin on the iron plate between the planks. In that bright light I could see the two Cubans in the front seat scrambling as the car drifted ass-first to one side. When the spinning rear wheel hit the planks, it bit into the wood and got instant traction. The driver overcorrected, and that wheel slid off the upstream edge of the bridge. I fired a second shot way over their heads and saw the front tires jerk sideways like they thought they could still back themselves out of trouble. The Escalade tilted, and the left front wheel went over the edge too. The whole thing hovered there for a second until it rolled off the bridge and splashed into the creek on its side. With the front windows open it sunk fast. When I could see the headlights under water, I snapped off the switch, and the spotlights dimmed out and the bridge went dark.

I walked down through the sagebrush out onto the bridge. Harvey's homemade abutments kept the channel narrow, so the creekbed under the bridge was scooped out deep and the water was about to a man's head. The current pushed the Escalade under the bridge and wedged it there sideways against the I-beams of the railcar undercarriage with water boiling around it. I stood in the middle of the bridge with my rifle across my shoulder, watching the trailhead where the other car was waiting in the dark. Whoever was sitting up there wouldn't have a plan B right away. I could hear yelling in Spanish. One of those shooters still had his head above water. I thought I heard him yell *por favor*, but it was hard to make out over the rush of the creek and my Spanish was never very good anyway.

I made a little come-along motion with my hand and the headlights of the second car popped on. It rolled to the edge of the hill then crept down the road. I stood there in the headlights waiting for them, holding the .270 with the muzzle pointed in their direction now. The car was another SUV, a big black Ford Expedition. Reno car rentals must have been flat out of black Escalades. With their first car stuck and their trigger pals drowning under the bridge and no time to set the scene, I didn't figure they'd shoot me just then. The Expedition stopped and waited for a minute. Then the passenger door opened and lit up the interior long enough for me to see there was two of them. The door closed, and GQ sort of floated into the high beams, sage dust swirling around him. I walked to his end of the bridge and waited for him to come the rest of the way.

He looked cold in his Hawaiian shirt, but he had a big smile on his face. He got up close enough so I could smell the cigarette on his breath.

"Pretty slick, Slick," he said. He walked past me to the edge of the bridge and looked over. The headlights still glowed in the water. "That water looks cold."

"Colder than Miami Beach."

"You think we can get them out of there?"

"You're welcome to try. You got one still thrashing around like a trapped badger."

He shivered and lit a smoke and made a face. "There's more where they came from."

"I figured."

He looked around, sucking on his smoke. "So how did you figure we'd come at you like this?"

"'Cause you don't know any other way. Those boys in the creek didn't know that once they shot me and Lester, one of them would get shot before you scattered cash and meth crap all around my trailer."

GQ just laughed. "Very good," he said. "I told you you should work for me."

I kind of nodded at the Expedition. "That big fella is all you need."

"But Teófilo doesn't work for me," he said. "More like I work for him, *claro*? And he works for some people in Mexico you don't ever want to meet."

"You're in some deep shit then either way."

"We're born in deep shit, my friend," he said. "Me more than most, but you too. If you weren't, you hicks would have reported Dad's plane the day you found it."

He looked pretty sure of himself.

"How long have you had those lights rigged?"

"Couple of days."

"Amazing," he said. "How long to break 'em down so this just looks like some tourists took a wrong turn into the river?"

"Couple of minutes."

"Improvise and adapt," he said, "right?"

I didn't say anything.

"So where'd you fight, soldier?"

"Fallujah."

"Ah, Lallafallujah," he said. "Some bad shit." He waited like he was wanting me to say something more.

"Some folks said we fired on ambulances. My boys never did."

He looked at me like he didn't believe it. "Why the hell not?" He laughed. "Hell man, shoot 'em all. Shoot their babies and their mamas too." He looked down into the current at the Escalade. "No? I get it. You're a moral killer." The headlight glow faded out in the water, then went dark. "They'll appreciate that."

"I'm heading back. If you and the big guy want to try to cross this bridge, that's your business."

"I think we'll pass," he said. He flicked his cigarette out into the creek, and I left him there. He hollered at me when I was about halfway across.

"Hey, soldier. Will I see you again?"

I had to shout for him to hear. "Not if I see you first."

He laughed at that. He cupped his hands and hollered one last time. "So what did you do in the war, daddy?"

"Sniper."

I walked back up into the sagebrush and unclipped two of the spotlights and hauled them back to the tin shack. I'd fetch the other two and reel up the wire at first light. I could see the headlights of the Expedition turning around and flying up the hill, then flickering away down into the trees. They just left those other two in the creek.

Chapter Twelve

I snoozed for a few hours in the front room of the trailer, waking up now and then to look out the window toward the bridge. When I finally rousted out, it was still full dark and the moon had slipped behind the crest and it was cold. I went out to start catching and graining the horses. I haltered three that were standing by the gate and easy to catch, then went to fetch my lights while the rest of the stock wandered up from the creek to see what they were missing. When I walked back from the bridge with the last two halogen lights, dragging two hundred feet of wire behind me in the dirt, I saw a kerosene glow from inside the trailer. I stowed the lights in the tin shack and was coiling the wire when Lester hustled outside in his jacket.

"Coffee'll be ready in no time," he said.

I tried not to look too surprised and handed him a halter. We caught the rest of the stock and went to brushing and saddling. We had six horses and mules rigged with sawbucks and our saddle horses cinched up by dawn. When Lester went back up to the trailer, I slipped into the corral to see Dave Cathcart's colt. I stopped about ten feet away and let him walk up to me while I tied back the corral gate so the few head of saddle horses we'd be leaving behind could get back out to pasture while we were gone. I talked to him and rubbed his neck until Lester came outside with coffee cups in both hands.

"So what's the plan here?" he said.

"I don't know. Try to put things back the way they were, I guess."

He just nodded and drank his coffee. It was light enough I could see he had his Ruger .357 holstered on his belt. I caught him watching me freezer-bag about three times more grain than we'd usually take and set it out on the platforms. I took a piece of blue plastic tarp and folded it and set it out too. We went inside and ate cereal while the stock finished the grain in their feeders. After ten minutes we blew out the lamps, hoisted the packs, and lashed down our loads on the two lead mules, and hung bags and slings on the rest. I stowed the grain in the empty bags. Then we buckled on our chinks, swung our legs over, and rode out leading three apiece. If Harvey had drove in the yard before we disappeared, I don't know what we would have done. I don't think I had any lies left in me.

It doesn't matter what foolishness you're up to, there's nothing like heading up that canyon horseback early in the morning in the summer with the sun on your back and the peaks all around and the pack animals strung out behind you in the sagebrush and the rush of the creek close by. We didn't talk, but I could see Lester resting his rope hand on the butt of that Ruger. I don't think he cared what we were doing as long as we were doing something. To him it was another adventure, even if his heart was broke. We were heading up that little rise along the edge of the first meadow before anybody said a word.

"If GQ and his crew are gonna take it to us," he said, "how come we don't take it to them first?"

"They already tried last night." I told him about the Escalade in the creek. He interrupted so much it took longer to tell it than it did to do it. We were heading into the aspens before I finished.

"Was it still there this morning?"

"Yeap."

"Did you see any bodies?"

"I didn't get close enough to look."

"Shit-fire, Tommy. So how did you know their wheels would spin them right off the bridge once you hit 'em with the lights?"

"There was a little diesel got spilled on the steel plate."

"You are one diabolical sonofabitch," he said.

"Keep that in mind next time you take a swing at me."

"I know you could've tried some Special Forces tricks on me if you wanted," he said. "Ripped out my windpipe or something."

I didn't say anything.

"I'm just glad you know what we're doing here, old son," he said. "But next time, you wake me up."

"If there is a next time."

* * *

The trail narrowed down through the aspen, and we fell into single file and stopped talking for a while. I dug out Nora's satellite phone and called the sheriff's office saying I was a fisherman that found an SUV wedged under the Aspen Creek bridge above the campgrounds. The phone said it was seven twenty-eight. When we hit a two-track below the second meadow, Lester rode up abreast.

"You think they're still alive?" he asked.

"Probably not. That bother you?"

"Not a bit," he said. "It's exactly what the bastards did to Callie. Lemme see that phone."

I handed it to him. He turned it around a bit, held it next to the Rolex to compare the time, and handed it back.

"Where'd you get that sucker?" he asked.

"The lady lawyer."

"She's a hot one. Were those her undies hanging from the rearview yesterday?"

"I surely hope so."

I looked straight up to the head of the canyon. I could see the pass and the snowfield below the pass shaped like a V high in the distance waiting for us like it was waiting for the billionaire that day he followed the canyon west, that little saddle in the Sierra crest showing him the way. In about ten minutes the phone rang back with the county sheriff's number showing, but I didn't answer. It was an hour later when we heard a chopper rumbling up-canyon. We were in the boggy timber way above the second meadow so a pilot couldn't see us if we weren't moving, but we couldn't get a great look at the helicopter either.

"Sheriff's, you think?" Lester asked. He was squinting up through the tree canopy. That new little mule was dancing at the end of his string.

"Can't tell. Sort of looks like Tony Aguilar."

"Then I bet he's got Sarah riding shotgun, looking for our ass," he said. "Looking juicy in that tanktop."

"Could be." I dug that phone out again and called Nora's number to give her a heads-up. When she didn't answer I slipped it back in my saddle pocket, but Lester noticed right off.

"You got that look again," he said.

"They got all kinds of cell service in Mammoth. Straight to voicemail means Nora's either left or never got there."

We leaned into it to cover more ground as soon as the helicopter passed over, the empty pack bags flapping. We didn't stop till we were in the edge of the young aspen just below The Roughs. There was a nice breeze coming down from the Sierra crest, and we listened for any sound of a chopper before we headed out over that bare shale where there'd be no cover to hide ourselves. It wasn't long before we crested the notch at the Wilderness Area boundary. Lester was in front, and he nodded to the sign.

"No firearms beyond this point," he said. He patted that Ruger.

"It's a tad late for you to get all law-abiding on me, bud." I swatted the butt of the little mule and we kept on riding.

Another half hour put us at the forks where we let the stock have a good drink before we started climbing out of the tamarack into the cirque. It would be the last deep running water they'd get a chance at until the next day.

When we got to our old camp by the avalanche site, I swung off in the shadows of a twisted old juniper where we'd be hard to spot. I handed my horse to Lester and slipped the .270 out of the scabbard. I rested the rifle across the seat of my saddle and scanned the wreck through the scope.

"It look the same?" Lester asked.

"So far."

"See anybody?"

"Nope."

"That doesn't mean they're not up there," he said.

I kept the reticle on that bench for another couple of minutes, just watching. The big snowfield hadn't melted much in the three days since we'd been there. When I'd seen enough, I stowed the rifle and took my horse from Lester.

"That two-seventy doesn't give us much firepower," he said.

"Dad always said it depends on who's doing the firing."

"Well, deer hunting I seen you shovel shells into that thing quicker than Lee Harvey Oswald on the History Channel," he said. "You'd best be on your game."

"I'll try to be."

He patted the butt of the Ruger. "If they take it to us, I'm ready."

I swung back up on my horse. "You shoot that thing off the back of that mare, she'll spook sideways eighteen feet then bog her head and pile you in the rocks."

We rode up through the boulders and mahogany heading for the snowfield. With the three animals apiece it was slow going, but we just took our time. We were closing in on the two whitebark pines where we'd tied up before when we heard a chopper again. We were out in the open, and there was nothing to do but just stop and wait.

"Tony again?" Lester asked.

It got louder toward the north for a minute, then faded off.

"Most likely just the Marines."

We moved on up the trail, the rocks more wet with snowmelt than ever. Lester reined in at the whitebarks and looked up toward the wreck.

"No place to tie all these guys here," he said.

"I figured we'd camp on that grassy spot just past the plane."

He didn't look too sure about all that, but he put on his Ray-Bans and goosed that mare out onto the snow, game as hell just like always. She picked her way with a big black packhorse and the two mules staying in her tracks when he made a switchback and started to climb. I held my string back so as not to crowd them, and headed out when he was about a third of the way up. I followed in his tracks when they were solid and made new ones when they weren't. Lester stopped a couple of times to let his animals rest and get their bearings. When I finally got up to the wreck, he was already dismounted and tying his string in a hemlock thicket.

We picked out a campsite for ourselves down-trail from the horses, then unsaddled and hobbled them out on the new grass. I saw Lester pull Harvey's chainsaw out of one of the empty pack bags.

"Just in case," he said.

When we had the animals squared away, we looked over the wreck. It was just like we left it, with the bogus note still inside the cockpit. I took it and folded it up and stuck it in my pocket. I walked around the plane, poked it with my boot, and rocked the tail to see how easy it moved. The tail stuck out about chest-high now. Lester walked up behind me as I was running my hand over the wires and bolts. There was a little breeze, and the view down the canyon was as clear as it could be, way past the valley and out into Nevada where this plane had taken off the winter before. It must have been real pretty to fly over this country on a day like today. If there was another soul down in that canyon, we sure couldn't see them.

"So what are we doing here exactly?" he said.

"I was sort of thinking we might just take this sucker apart and pack it off the mountain like it was never here."

Lester thought about that for a minute then sort of laughed.

"Yeah," he said. "I get where you're going. They take the body, so we take the plane. We see 'em and raise 'em. I don't know if we got enough stock, though."

"Six is all we got, so we'll see how much plane is left after six loads. How much you figure the motor weighs?"

"Too much to put in one pack bag, that's for damn sure. We'd need an elephant." He walked back up to the nose where it was balancing on the rock and the bent-over pine and opened the cowling, just studying things for a bit and not saying a word.

"If I stripped the block clean, that would make about a hundred-pound load, give or take," he said. "Then we could balance that out with the heads, the crank, and the pistons, all the other heavy stuff in the other bag. Old Reverend Al could pack that out easy."

We studied the black gelding cropping grass. He was sixteen hands and thirteen hundred pounds, and earned his keep every summer hauling big loads or truly fat people that had no business horseback.

"I wouldn't want to sore him up."

"A tight little squaw hitch will keep it riding high," Lester said. "I've hauled two hundred pounds of salt blocks on him for Becky Tyree."

"But that's over flat ground."

"He'll be okay. That sucker's game."

"How long will it take you to break down the engine?"

"Till dark. Probably way longer."

"Then let's get to it."

In the beginning I helped Lester. He had a good socket set and the fresh can of Liquid Wrench to unbolt that motor from the mounts, but mostly we just tore into things, ripping off the cowling, cutting belts and hoses with knives and hacksaws, and generally making a mess.

"It ain't like we got to put the sonofabitch back together," he said. He tossed one of the heads in the dirt.

I fetched a couple of buckets of sandy granite from under the trees. When we were finally about to roll the block out, I dragged a piece of blue tarp and spread it next to the cowling. When crankcase oil started dripping down on the plastic I was ready with the sand, pouring it on the tarp to soak it up.

"You musta been plotting this out for days in that sick brain of yours," Lester said. "This is sooo Tommy Smith." He took a pinch of Copenhagen.

It was all greasy hands and skinned knuckles for the next hour or so, me pretty much doing what Lester told me.

"Hand me that seven-sixteenth," he said.

I handed it to him.

"I hate machinery."

"You should quit the horseback life," he said, "and go to aircraft mechanic school. You're a natural."

"Screw you. Valves and springs and cams. It's worse than being back in Mister Hessell's auto shop class."

"I'm handled here," he said. "Why don't you go tear into that sucker. Break something. You'll feel better."

I wiped my hands and whacked away at the door with a hammer and cold chisel. It popped off quick. The other door was under the wreck where I couldn't get to it. Then I lowered myself down and started on the insides, unscrewing the instrument panel, unbolting the stick, cutting wires, and dismantling the cockpit from the inside out. I was careful not to touch the dried blood on the panel when I lifted out the radio and such. I kept finding little things we didn't pay attention to before, like an Auto Club map of Nevada, a prescription bottle for Ibuprofen, a couple of empty cardboard fruit drinks with the straws still in them, and a critter-chewed Cheetos bag. Unbolting the seats took a while because it was so cramped in there and they were laying sideways, but they stacked up nice once I got them out with the hammer and chisel. I'd hauled a lot of junk out, but from outside the plane still looked about the same.

I took a break and tended to the stock, stringing out two separate picket lines for the night and giving everybody a pile of grain on the grass when they got restless. There was snowmelt trickling down through the rocks from up toward the pass. I pulled some stones out to make a catch basin a couple of feet across and watched it fill up enough for a horse to drink out of so we wouldn't have to walk them halfway down the mountain before we turned in.

Lester was still humming along pulling the pistons. Give him a job like that, he's set for hours. I built a fire near the plane and heated up a can of Dinty Moore stew we could eat while we worked. While I watched the pot, I handed Lester the old Cheetos bag.

"The hell?"

"Appetizers."

"All his money and he's eating Cheetos like some damn kid," he said.

"They don't have a separate section in the AM-PM says snack food for billionaires."

He crumpled up the bag and tossed it in the fire. "Give me some of them caviar Cheetos," he said, "with that chewy caviar goodness."

It was close to the longest day of the year, so we had daylight for a long time. When it finally got too dusky to see inside the cockpit, I lit the Colemans, poured us some Crown Royal, and went back to helping Lester on the motor. We kept working by lamplight until he had the block picked clean and cams, and pans, and rods, and pistons, the drive shaft, heads, and a slew of bolts piled up on the blue tarp. The Nevada hills off east started to get a silver glow, and pretty soon the moon came up just about full. We were sitting a couple of thousand feet above the rim of the hills, so it looked like the moon was rising below us at our feet. When I got up I saw Tower Peak all lit up silver and black now off to the west.

"We got enough to balance out the block with this mess," Lester said. "It'll be about all that big black sucker can pack, though."

I filled a can from my catch basin and heated water so we could wash the grease off our hands. We watered the stock one at a time, picketed them on the lines, and saw to our bedrolls. That all took a long time. We sat there for a bit on our tarps then, drinking Crown Royal and watching the row of horses and mules standing quiet in the moonlight and the big pile of junk lying next to the plane.

"It's like we're at the top of the world," he said.

"We kind of are. Man, I'm whipped."

"You're never whipped."

"Well, I'm whipped tonight." I pulled off my boots and crawled into my bedroll. I called Nora again, but it was right to voicemail like before. I left a message but didn't talk loud.

"Hey Nora. Just wanted to make sure you're safe in Mammoth and not gallivanting around out in the open.

Call me a-s-a-p. Don't matter how late. *Doesn't* matter how late. Shit."

I tucked the phone under the rolled-up jacket I was using for a pillow.

"You worried about her?" Lester asked.

"I wish I wasn't, but yeah."

I flattened out in the bedroll with the tarp open. It was a mild night, even at ten thousand feet.

"Say, Tommy?"

I was half dozing.

"You think Callie's in heaven?"

"Sure, Lester."

"You believe in heaven?"

"Not really."

"Why not? The war?"

"I don't know. I just don't spend a lot of time thinking about things like that."

"Well, right now I got to think there is," he said.

"I know. Makes sense for you."

"It doesn't really make sense at all though, even when I want it to. I watched too much goddamn *Nova* in high school."

"Goodnight, Lester."

I was awake now. I kept opening my eyes to see all that moonlit broken country down below, and the animals on the picket line, and the peaks all huge above us. I caught myself memorizing things and made myself stop.

"You asleep?" he asked.

"Yes."

"After someone dies, you believe in closure?"

"I believe there's no such thing."

He was quiet for a bit except for some snuffling like maybe he was crying for Callie Dean. I snuck a look over. He was laying on his back staring at the moon. It looked close enough to hit with a rock.

"In the moonlight the plane looks like some spacecraft crashed on Mars," he said. "You ever think about outer space?"

"Not ever."

"You see those movies with guys standing all alone on some distant planet a gazillion miles out in deep space with some weird moon on the horizon. But what if we're the ones on the distant planet and all this just over our heads is deep space, all cold and huge and empty? You ever think that lying here we're flying a million miles an hour in outer space right now?"

"One of us is, that's a fact."

Lester got quiet. After a bit a breeze kicked up and woke me, and I saw sparks from the fire swirling around between us and the plane. That was strange. I remembered summer nights in the Sierra as almost always dead still.

I didn't wake up until the sun was up and Lester was shaking fuel from the chainsaw on a pile of pine chunks to start a fire. The stock was already watered and hobbled out on the grass with piles of grain, and I could see he'd already been working on the wreck. He threw a kitchen match on the pine and the gas blazed up.

"You're a regular woodsman, bud. Old John Muir'd be proud of you."

"Well, look who's among the living," he said. "I thought you were going to sleep for a week."

Lester was ready with the coffee pot to set on the wire grill to boil.

"You just lay there and get your beauty rest," he said. "Lunch'll be ready before you know it."

I got up and pissed. The air was breezy and almost warm, like there was a storm coming. There wasn't much to do after I gathered more firewood but watch Lester cook breakfast. He had some bacon and runny pancakes going before long and kept opening the lid of the coffeepot.

"A watched pot never boils. Didn't your mom tell you that?"

"We're up too damn high, is what," he said.

After breakfast we went back to work on the plane. We popped the rear flaps off the tail then hacksawed the whole section off. I wrote the numbers on the tail and wing down in my tallybook, then we swapped ends and Lester went to work on the cowling. I crawled in to see what I'd missed the night before. A bunch of flies were pasted to the inside of the windshield like the headliner of a pickup if you've left the windows down and rain is coming. I popped the spot welds on one gas tank with a chisel and started to hacksaw the galvanized neck of the tank but thought better of it. It was so cramped in there I had to get out. Pretty soon we were down to the fuselage and the one wing, just tubing and fabric with the nose cut back to the windshield. With it stripped down like that, it did kind of look like some spaceship. We rocked it back and forth until we got it upright, then we unbolted the struts and started sawing off the wing with a hacksaw.

"Get the gravy," Lester said, "we're down to the dark meat."

I broke a hacksaw blade when I was about through the last piece of tubing, and we just twisted the wing till it came off.

"Still blows me away how flimsy this sucker is," he said. He tossed a strut into a pile.

"We'll, let's get this mess mantied up."

We started sorting the pieces into pack loads, the heavy stuff like the motor into paired pack bags, the big awkward junk like wingflaps, doors, and the seats buckled into slings. We'd pick up one bag then the other to keep the weight as even as we could. We separated out the long or awkward pieces like the prop. We'd tie those across the tops of the loads at the very last. We'd done this together so many times we didn't have to say much. Pretty soon we had the place pretty well cleared off and six piles of airplane ready to pack.

"Well, Einstein," Lester said, "we definitely got more plane than we got mules."

We just looked at that gutted fuselage and wing.

"Yeah. We need another four animals and twenty more hacksaw blades."

"And another full day," he said. "You got any other bright ideas?"

I walked around the fuselage. "Grab an end. Let's see if we can pull it away from that tree."

We wiggled the wreck again so nothing was snagged, and dragged it off the rock outcropping. It was awkward, but we were stout boys and could almost lift it.

"Where to?" Lester asked.

"That sandy spot."

We wrestled it over about ten feet. It rested thirty feet off the trail.

"You want to haul it into the trees?"

"Couldn't if we wanted to. Best keep it away from the trees."

"How come?" he asked.

"We're going to blow it up."

"The hell."

Lester looked at me like I was crazy. I walked over to where the pack loads were stacked and dug out the high-way map. Lester watched me unfold it, then twist it and roll it into a long ropey thing. I walked around the wreck and unscrewed a gas cap.

"There's no gas left," he said. "Remember?"

"There's fumes."

"You'll need more than that, son."

I shoved the twisted paper into the neck of the closest tank like a fuse.

"Go ahead and light it," he said. "See if I'm right."

"Let's tie up the stock just in case."

"Dreamer," he said.

Lester helped me unhobble and lead the animals back to the picket line. When they were all tied snug, he followed me back to the wreck. I bent down and sniffed for gas but barely got a whiff. The breeze blew out a couple of matches before I got the rolled-up map to catch fire. I scampered back about thirty feet.

"Lester?"

I motioned him to step away from the plane. He waved me off like usual but moved back a few steps just in case. We watched it from opposite sides of the wreck for a minute, but nothing happened. Lester was about to say something when there was a big pop, kind of hollow and tinny like from inside the gas tank as the whole plane exploded and caught fire in an instant. Just like that. Lester jumped back and fell on his butt and scrambled away from the fire. A couple of the horses flinched on the picket line. The little mule just looked sideways at us like she was saying, What else you got? Lester looked at me like a crazy man through the flames, orange and wispy and shimmering with the heat.

"Damn," he said. "There is like *no* smoke."

"That's good. Nobody'll spot it then."

"Damn." He just stared at the flames.

"Let's grab that wing."

We hoisted the wing and tossed it on the fire. Then we sat on the ground and ate our lunch while the fire burned.

"How'd you know it'd do that? How'd you know it would just explode and burn with nothing but the fumes?"

"I don't know. I just kinda figured it might."

It burned for a good twenty minutes. Pretty soon all that was left was a black frame of bent-up tubing.

"Those old ponies hardly flinched," he said.

"They're around gunfire every fall."

We rolled our bedrolls and stowed the kitchen gear and waited for the fire to die out. When we were about ready to pack up, I walked over to the frame and stuck my hand out. The tubing was already cool to the touch. I looked to see how much of the ground we'd singed and it wasn't too bad.

"Come on, Lester. Let's find a hole to hide this sucker."

We split up and walked though the crushed granite and boulders and clusters of whitebark pine and snow-bent hemlock. About a hundred feet south of our camp downslope in some scattered pine and boulders I found a drop-off in a granite slab that made a slot in the rocks about ten feet deep. Gray twigs and limbs of dead trees were scattered on the ground and smears of lichen gave the granite a blotchy green and orange look. No human being, even going back to the Piute hunters, had probably ever looked down into that slot because there was no reason to meander over there with the natural pass so close. Even where we camped was not a spot anybody else would choose. There was better water down-trail on our side of the pass, and Little Meadow was just over the crest about thirty minutes walk on the other side.

We dragged the skeleton of the fuselage over the rocks and into the trees. A couple of the horses spooked on the picket line as we stumbled along near them, but the mules didn't pay us any mind. Even if it wasn't heavy, the frame was awkward to carry over rough ground and we set it down once to catch our breath in the thin air.

"Damn," Lester said. "We're just erasing this guy right off the face of the earth."

We dragged the frame the rest of the way to the edge of the slot and dropped it in. It wedged about halfway to the bottom, but if you stood five feet back from the edge you couldn't see it. Lester brought the wing over next and we used that to tamp the fuselage down another couple of feet, then we tossed the wing on top.

"Well that's that," he said. "Nobody's gonna find this puppy now."

"I sure hope not."

"Why a chopper could fly right over and never see it."

Before we saddled up we scoured our camp. I scuffed the burned spots on the ground as best I could with my boot, then I had Lester help me rake up the manure and scatter it on the ground where we'd burned the plane to cover the singed spots. I dropped some at the crash site to cover any oil drips.

"The birds will peck and scratch through the horse turds for the seeds and make this look just as natural as can be."

"You are so weird," he said.

"One good rain, you'll never know anything was here."

Lester lifted his head up and sniffed the air for the coming storm like a dog. We started saddling up the eight animals at the picket lines, brushing them good before we set the saddle pads on so we wouldn't have any sore backs when we got back on down the mountain.

"What're we going to do with all this junk?" Lester asked.

"I was hoping you had some ideas." I set my rig on my horse, smoothing my pads and Navajo, brushing dirt off the cinch, buckling the rifle scabbard on the off-side. For a minute there, I didn't do anything but just stare at the smooth brass of the rigging plate and run my hands over the oak-leaf tooling that Dad kept oiled up so well.

"Anytime now," Lester said.

He was hoisting a pack bag onto one of the mules. I snapped out of it and went to load the other side. We took our time getting all six animals loaded up. The first mile would be steep and I didn't want any packs shifting on us. We used diamond hitches or squaw hitches depending on the load. About the hardest piece to pack was the tail section. We tied it on its side on top of the roan where it cantilevered out over his butt with a few inches to spare. If he was a spooky horse, we sure as hell would have found out then. We packed the big black horse last, so he wouldn't have to stand around under all the weight any longer than he had to. The bags carrying the motor were so damned heavy we each hefted one at the same time, resting them against his sides to give us each a free hand, then slipping the straps over the sawbucks one after the other as we eased the weight from us to him. He gave a grunt as the whole thing settled.

"This is a *load*," Lester said. "Reverend Al says we're discriminating."

"Cut it out." It came out more snappish than I'd meant.

"Look," he said. "I know we wouldn't have to do all this if I hadn't swiped the damn watch. This is all because of me."

"Bullshit. These folks are scum. Nobody could see this coming. You're not in their league, bud. You never meant nothing bad."

"But you wouldn't have done it," he said.

"That ain't the point. That dead body was worth millions to one side when it was here and millions to the other when it was gone. Somebody was bound to take it to us one way or another once we found it, and not lost a wink of sleep either."

"Well."

"Well nothing, Lester. Forget it."

We tarped the load, threw a squaw hitch, and snugged down the lashrope good and tight. I took one last look around the campsite, hoping we hadn't forgot anything obvious. A person would have to look pretty hard to ever think a plane had crashed on that bench. Even the little whitebark pine was just bent but not broken off. A wind was starting to kick up.

"Let's string them up and get the hell out of here," Lester said.

I looked down that snowfield then back to those horses and mules with their crazy top-heavy loads. Even the little new mule was standing quiet like she knew today she wouldn't have any energy to waste.

"I don't know. Steep as that is, we tie 'em together and one of them pulls back or stumbles in the snow, we got ourselves one hell of a wreck."

"You got a better idea?" he asked.

"I'm going to lead my horse down on foot. When I get to the bottom, you take these guys and turn 'em loose one at a time after me. I'll catch 'em as they come down. That way they can keep their balance and go their own pace."

I hung my bridle on the saddle horn and led my horse by the *mecate* down the snowfield. I took it slow and let him pick his footing. He stopped once right on top of me when I slipped on my ass on an icy spot. It took me a few minutes to make it down. I led him over into some trees twenty feet off the trail and tied him tight, then signaled Lester to send the rest of them on down.

He led the string one at a time to the edge of the snowfield, starting with the black gelding. Lester slipped each leadline up through the hitches so they wouldn't drag before he turned them loose. He knew his business. He had that string coming down in the order we would be leading them. I watched until all six of them were picking their way down at liberty, their heads low, balancing the big loads on their backs as they came, taking one slow step at a time through the snow, following the path of the one before. They made a big sweeping S curve as they switch-backed across the snowfield. It was about the prettiest thing I ever saw.

Chapter Thirteen

I caught them up one at a time, tying the first horse to a pine then stringing the lead of the next one through the ring on the britchen and tying it off. When I looked up, I saw Lester stopped about halfway down, watching. Then he led his horse the rest of the way. The wind was gusting now and thunder rumbled in the distance. Damned if I didn't see snow closing in on the high peaks. He stepped aboard the mare, and I handed him his string.

"That was downright impressive," he said.

"Too bad all we know how to do is pack."

I bridled my horse, grabbed my string, and swung up. Lester led the way as we headed down further into the cirque leading three animals apiece. We hadn't gone more than a few hundred yards when I hollered for him to stop. I'd been watching the tail section on my lead horse, the big roan. I dismounted and checked the load. The tail flaps had been built to rotate on two little stubs of three-quarter inch steel tube about an inch long. The stubs were rusty now, and the whole set-up looked like it had been built in somebody's garage. The underside stub had been rubbing on the roan's rump, so I reset the thing best I could. By now the first big drops of rain hit, and I pulled my slicker from under the tarp of the roan before I mounted. After a few minutes of getting pelted, Lester untied his slicker from behind his cantle and pulled it on as he rode. It snapped around in the wind, and Harvey's mare didn't like it much.

We made steady time, letting the two lead pack horses set the pace. They didn't see much sense dawdling so far from their home corral and pasture. The little mule was just in front of me at the end of Lester's string and even she kept slack in her lead, not wanting to be left behind. When we got close to our trail-mending camp from the week before, Lester turned off into the rocks where the creek tumbled down and we let the stock get a good drink. I got off and reset the tail section again on the roan.

"Should've burned that with the other stuff," he said.

"You're dead right on that. He's already wore some of the hair off."

I stepped back up and Lester led the way down toward the forks in the rain. It was coming steady now, and visibility down-canyon was only a couple of miles. I looked back toward the site of the wreck, and it was already half-hidden in white snow flurries. We rode without talking, hunkered down under our hats and collars. The trail wound into scattered trees and big boulders with new grass on either side. I looked back at the roan again.

"Pull up, Lester."

I got off and we tied up. I loosened the lashrope on the roan, and Lester helped me lift the tail section off him. The tailflap stub had worn a sore on his butt about the size of an Eisenhower dollar.

"Sonofabitch." I looked over to a boulder as tall as a man about twenty feet off the trail. "Over here, bud."

We carried that thing over and stashed it behind the rock. The tail stood four feet high, so a person couldn't see it from the trail, but we didn't try to hide it much. We retied the roan's hitch with that wet lashrope then just stood there in the rain for a second looking at the rocks. Lester gave a what-the-hell shrug and we mounted up. The rain had eased off to just a drizzle.

We were just coming to the forks and were clopping along in sight of the snow cabin when I saw the blood on Lester's back a second before I heard the shots. The red on his yellow slicker looked like catsup on mustard, all wet in the rain. He kept on riding, sitting up more rigid than usual. I hollered for him to pull up as I jumped off and ran around his string to get to him. Four more shots popped right in a row and I felt one zip just overhead.

"Jesus, Tommy," was all Lester said. I dragged him out of his saddle and walked him toward the rocks. When we had some cover, I let him fall on his knees and I peeled back the slicker. It was hard to tell with his shirt on, but it looked like he'd been hit high in the back above the shoulder blade. A full automatic burst hit the top of the rocks, spraying us with granite chips.

"Oh shit shit shit," Lester said, like it took all the energy he had left.

I shushed him and we listened. There wasn't a sound. The two pack strings just stopped, eight animals in single file on the narrow trail. They would stand for about a minute glad for the rest, then head on down the road. Quicker if the shooting got close. I propped Lester with his back against a rock.

"Lean back and keep some pressure on it till I see what's what."

"You ain't gonna leave me here?"

"Just to tie up the horses and fetch my rifle. You stay put."

Through the branches you could see the little tower sticking up from the snow cabin from where we were hunkered down. It was just a plank box, about as big as an old-fashioned phone booth. It used to have a ladder in it to climb in and out of the cabin like an escape hatch when the snow was higher than the roof. I crouched and snuck to Lester's horse and tied her to a tamarack, then tied off the black gelding to his saddle horn. I did the same with my string. That would hold them for a few more minutes unless they got spooked. I pulled the .270 from the scabbard and grabbed the fresh box of cartridges, the first-aid kit, and the Crown Royal from my saddle pockets. I stayed low between two big pack loads, watching and listening. They must not have had a good shot at me or they would have taken one then. Most likely the shooter was on the move, getting a closer spot. The drizzle dulled down any noise except the sound of the horses and mules shifting their weight, which was really no sound at all. I hustled back to where I'd left Lester and handed him the Crown Royal.

"My pard," he said. He sounded weak.

"How you doing?"

He tried a grin, but his face was white.

"Okay," he said. "Feels weird. I never been shot before."

"You'll be sore as hell in the morning."

"I'm not gonna to die?"

"It's a long way from your heart, bud. Well, not that long, actually. A long way from your mouth, anyway."

He took a sip of the Crown Royal. "He knows where I am, don't he," he said. He was almost panting.

"We want him to. There'll be two of 'em. This way I can find them easier."

"You're using me for bait?"

"Yeah. Just while I check out the neighborhood."

I inspected the breech, uncapped the scope, and wiped the lens with the end of my neck rag. Then I went hunting. I stayed in the tamarack as I worked my way down-trail of the stock. When I got a ways below Lester, I took off my slicker and spread it over a bough of a white fir then kept moving on down. When I made it near the snow cabin I parked myself in some timber with a good view of the open country to the north where I figured the shot came from, but stayed hid from the cabin by a tree. At least one of these boys would be up there in the rocks, as it was an easy climb with a clear field of fire. I waited a long time, just listening for any sound over the steady rumble of the creek off behind me. Finally there was a clatter of rock up on the opposite slope, but it was far off and faint and I couldn't see movement. I wanted to get back to Lester pretty quick before his patience wore out.

"Up here, asshole," somebody shouted way up the slope. Even far off you could pick up the accent. I just waited. He shouted again like he wanted my attention up there, not anywhere else. I braced against the tree bark and swept that hillside with my scope, breaking it into quadrants until I found him, another Cuban from the look of him. He was focusing down at the pack string with binoculars, hiding in the rocks above a screen of trees waiting for one of us to show. He wouldn't want to wait too long, but if he knew about his *compañeros* in the creek two nights before he'd be cautious and looking for tricks, maybe afraid to come too close. On the other hand he was a city boy outside in the rain. I looked over the top of the scope to memorize the patch of ground with just my eyes. Once I knew where to look, I could spot the guy easy without the scope. Then I turned sideways around that tree and squeezed off a round into the escape tower on the snow cabin. I felt better then. I was only about a hundred fifty feet off and could hear a thump and a clatter.

"Tommy?" It was Lester.

I hustled across the trail below the pack strings and climbed into the timber on the other side. A full automatic pop-pop-pop-pop rattled down from the Cuban in the rocks, and I could see the horses scamper, pulling back. The little mule dropped, and the big buckskin mule she was tied to started dancing in place in front of where she lay. The whole string was looking to stampede out of there. I heard Lester shout again but couldn't make it out. Then it was quiet again. The guy in the rocks was out of his element and acting frustrated. He only shot at the animals to see something get hit. I gained altitude then settled into some rocks under the pines and fixed on the guy's sniper nest before I put the scope on him. I waited for him to finally rise up and try to sneak down toward Lester. The closer he got, the more he hurried. He wasn't wearing a hat, only a jacket and shorts. He carried a short little bullpup weapon with an interior barrel, probably a P90. They were half plastic and didn't look any more dangerous than a staple-gun. I had him from the side, almost from behind. When he stopped to steady himself to fire, I shot him and he fell. I walked back down to the snow cabin, circling around to the down-trail side where the door faced. I stopped and watched it for a minute, not making a sound, just listening. The door wasn't dangling open like it had for fifty years, but it was sprung so bad it wouldn't close all the way. I walked up to the cabin as quiet as I could. I held the Remington on the door and pushed it to the side with my foot. Inside I could see a new lace-up boot dangling down and some sock and bare leg and traces of blood on the dirt.

Then the cabin wall exploded with splinters and chunks of wood and a blast of automatic fire and my face burned like crazy. Before I could think I'd taken a knee and fired twice up into the shooter's hiding place in the escape tower. An AK-47 dropped on the dirt and I stopped shooting. More blood dripped down. I stepped partway inside the cabin. I could see a whole leg hanging down now, but that sucker was stuck up there pretty good. More blood had dripped all over my right boot and I stepped back. That stopped me till I figured the blood was mine. My cheek was stinging and wet. I felt around and pulled a sharp chunk of pine plank big enough to use for kindling from that fleshy spot just in front of my ear. If I hadn't been wearing my hat and studying the ground the splinters from that blast would have ripped out my eyes. I peeked up into the escape tower just to be sure that bastard was dead then hustled back to Lester. By then the rain had stopped.

I grabbed my slicker from the fir on the way back. It had a bullet hole in the sleeve and the round had tore a yellow furrow in the tree bark. The edge that spreads behind the saddle over a horse's butt was just tatters. When I got to the pack string, the little mule was down on her forelegs with her head sideways on the trail and her rump in the air wedged against a rock so she couldn't fall over. I crouched down next to Lester and peeled back his slicker.

"Jesus, Tom." He looked pretty scared when he saw my face.

"Just wood splinters. I got careless."

"Did you kill the bastard?"

"Eventually."

"I feel like I'm gonna puke," he said.

"That's okay. Might make you feel better. You're in shock. Let's lay you down."

I looked for an exit hole but that small-bore round was still inside him somewhere, maybe behind a bone. I started field-dressing the wound.

"I heard the shooting," he said. He rolled forward to make it easier for me. "I was scared shitless."

"It's over for now. Any blood in your spit?"

"No. How come?"

"Want to be sure the bullet didn't nick a lung."

That made him look sicker. "But you got him, right?"

"There was two of them. The one who shot you from up there. The second one in the snow cabin. That's the one almost got me."

"But you got them," he said.

"Yeah."

"That one bastard shot Harvey's new mule," he said. "There go our summer wages."

"Does that hurt?"

"Not so bad," he said. "Are you sure that bastard shot me is dead?"

"He's dead."

"Did you check?"

"I don't need to check."

"Did you shoot him in the head?"

"What do you think?"

"Did you take his machine gun?"

"No. Lie still for christsakes."

"Why not? It's got to be way more gun than your deer rifle."

"That fact, although pertinent, did not do that sucker a hell of a lot of good."

Lester just tried to laugh.

"Besides, we got to leave things as-is, submachine guns and all. Like a crime scene. Shooting Lester Wendover out of season has got to be plumb illegal. At least some sort of misdemeanor."

"The second guy was in the snow cabin? The one that shot you."

"He didn't shoot me. He shot the door. I was in the way."

"But he was in the cabin?"

"Yeah."

"How did you know he'd be there?"

"Because he was a city boy and it was the only building in the damn Wilderness."

"Did you see him either?" Lester asked.

"Just his feet. He's stuck up in there like Santa Claus. He just wasn't quite as dead as he might have been." I tore the backing off a big butterfly bandage. "When you don't see them through the scope, you never know for sure." Lester always liked hearing the technical stuff, and I figured it would keep his mind off his hurt.

"How'd you know there was two of 'em?"

"Jesus, you're chatty today."

"Well, I want to know," he said. "How did you figure there were two?"

"He wouldn't send somebody this far into the back country alone."

"GQ?"

"His *jefe*. Teófilo."

"How do you know there ain't no more?"

"There's probably more waiting around the pack station. But sending two ATV's up-canyon makes sense."

"How do you know they rode ATVs?"

"Because they ain't the kind to walk."

"Motor vehicles up here are illegal," he said.

"Then that's why I shot 'em." I pulled a wood sliver out of my neck rag that was scratching me under the chin. "Quit talking for chrissakes."

"Would I know all this shit if I'd been in the army?"

"Probably not."

I pulled Lester's shirt up around his neck. I eased his slicker back over his shoulders and closed up the first-aid kit. It was designed for camp burns and cuts and such, but it would have to do for now.

"They'll be waiting for us at the pack station then," he said.

"So we won't go to the pack station."

"Aspen Pass to Boundary Lake, then down the old switchbacks to Henry Lake," he said, "then out at the Summers Lake trailhead. They're not local, so they won't have a clue."

"See. You're smarter than you think you are. There's lots of ways out if you know the country."

"We know the country," he said.

I left him and hurried over to the stock, taking my knife out as I went. The buckskin mule tied in front of the dead mule was pulling sideways trying to get free. He'd pulled the dead mule's wet leadrope so tight I had to cut it. That quieted him down. I cut the lashrope to pull her tarp off and drag the slings off her. I unbuckled the slings around a gas tank, a door, Harvey's chainsaw and the two airplane seats. When I jostled her I could see where the round smashed into her just behind her left eye. It was a high-penetration round made to pierce body armor. The heat was escaping her rained-on hide almost like steam, and she was already starting to stiffen up. She would have grown into a good little mule. She'd carried that crazy load with no complaints. I left the chainsaw on a rock and stashed the other stuff deep in the pines so there'd be no trace of the wreck left on the trail. Somebody might find that junk someday, but not till this whole mess was over.

I got Lester to his feet and took the Crown Royal bottle from him so he wouldn't drop it when we walked back to the horses. I steadied him, but he was still buckaroo enough to get on his horse by himself, even with a hole in his back. We left his slicker on him to keep him warm. I dallied the black gelding's lead once around Lester's saddle horn and set his hand on it, then turned his mare around. I stowed the whisky and got aboard myself. Then I rode around to the front of the line and headed us back over to the crossing.

I left Lester mounted while I led the black horse right up next to the creek and unpacked him. There was a wide spot in the creekbed with a hole against the bank where the grass was high and the water deep and slow moving. After I stripped the tarp I muscled the bags up high enough to free the straps from the sawbucks then let the bags drop to the ground. I dumped the engine block and rolled it to the bank and pushed it into the creek. It sat there in four feet of water but with the reflection on the surface ripples, a person couldn't see it unless they were standing right over it. I dragged the second bag with the pistons and the rest of the junk to the bank and dumped that in too.

"Now who's John goddamn Muir." Lester sat his horse watching me. "Freakin' litterbug."

I dropped to my knees on the creek bank and washed the side of my face with that cold water for a couple of minutes until it numbed up. When I got up, I stuffed the rope and tarp into the empty bags and hung them back on the black horse. He looked relieved to get that load off. Then I tied him and the buckskin mule into my string.

"I figure every time we get to a likely spot we'll unload more of this. Time we get to Boundary Lake that plane will have flat disappeared. You lead the way, bud. Let's get the hell off this trail."

"To Aspen Pass?"

"To Aspen Pass."

Lester rode out and the rest of us followed. We took the south fork of the trail and forded the creek at the wide shallow crossing under the trees, then headed upslope into the rocks and timber toward Aspen Pass. About ten minutes along I hollered for Lester to stop on an uphill grade, and I unpacked the rest of the load from the roan, tossing a bunch of cockpit hardware down a ravine behind a little ridge above the trail. Folks in the backcountry whether afoot or horseback are packing weight. They go from point to point and mostly don't waste any effort sightseeing off-trail except from their camps.

"That radio's probably worth some coin," Lester said.

"Well, once you're on the mend we'll ask Harvey to borrow even more of his animals, and we'll ride back here and fetch it down to the swap meet in Carson City. Fair enough?"

"Fair enough," he said.

"How you doing up there?"

"I'm a little drunk," he said.

"Well, you'll sleep in a hospital bed tonight."

I wrote down in my tallybook where we'd dumped the instruments with the bloodstains in case we ever needed to prove the old boy had died. Lester rode on up through the boulders and pines, and I followed. I pulled out Nora's phone and tried her again. I didn't figure she'd answer, and when she didn't I called Sarah Cathcart. The dispatcher said she'd get Sarah to call me back, and I gave her the number. I was unpacking the prop from another mule up near the top of the pass when she called.

"Hey, stranger."

"Tommy, what the heck are you up to? Harvey's fit to be tied. Where are you?"

"Above the forks. Lester's got shot."

"Oh god, Tommy."

"He'll be okay. He'll need a medevac, though."

"Who shot him?"

"Your boyfriend GQ's Cubans. Like the fellas you fished out of the Escalade yesterday morning."

Even over that phone I could hear her tisk and sigh like a schoolteacher.

"I figured you'd know all about that," she said.

"I'm the one that called it in."

"I figured that too," she said. "You know better than to leave the scene of an accident."

"And you know it wasn't no accident. They both dead?"

"One survived," she said. "He might have brain damage from loss of oxygen."

"That'd be a shame."

"Tommy, you're no dealer. Why are these idiots shooting at you?"

"It wasn't just Callie bullshitting. We found the missing plane. GQ's dad. We found it six days ago."

"And you didn't tell me? My god, Tommy."

"Things got out of control quick once Callie and Lester tried to play old Gerald for money."

"So there was never any drugs."

"Nope."

"Gerald is flying up to the head of Aspen Canyon right about now in a Reno Action News chopper," she said. "He says he found the wreck with proof his dad survived."

"He's lying. You know that much."

I told her that GQ's crew lifted the body and left a fake note, then aimed for us after they killed Callie and Albert, so we lifted the plane on them.

"I figured once his version of the story fell apart on TV, he'd be too busy to bother us."

"You have totally lost your mind," she said. "What am I going to do with you? That Caddie in the creek was stocked like an armory. Mitch saw stuff even he'd never seen before."

"Mind he doesn't swipe a P90. He might hurt himself."

"He'll be too busy gunning for you," she said. "Are you sure Les is okay?"

I told her that the Cubans had caught us up at the forks. I told her I'd call her back as soon as I got us to a safe place for a chopper to land at Boundary Lake.

"I'll tell you the rest when I see you."

"I hate to ask. Did the shooters get away?"

"No they didn't."

"Okay," she said. "Okay."

"There'll be a couple more waiting by the pack station, Sarah, and they got better weapons than you, so you look sharp and don't even think of driving back up there alone."

5

"I won't."

"And tell Harvey to stay away, too. Tell him it's a law enforcement problem."

"I will," she said. "I don't know if he'll listen."

"I'm not fooling. Things aren't working out for GQ. His guys are blasting everything that moves. Covering their tracks. I wouldn't want to be in his boots after today."

"Okay."

"Have you seen that lawyer Nora Ross?"

"No," she said. "Should I?"

"You best want to find her."

"Okay," she said.

"I gotta go keep Lester moving. I'll call you soon."

"Okay. Tommy? Don't let anything happen to you."

"Nothing's happening to me."

I stashed the phone and climbed on my horse. Lester led us on up the trail.

By the time we hit Aspen Pass then cleared the timber I had unloaded and hid the last of the plane and it started to rain again. The billionaire's friends and his family could look a long time and never find a trace now. We had our beds and kitchen on the buckskin mule, but the rest of the animals were traveling light so I'd put him at the head of the string to let him set the pace. Beyond the pass, the trail broke out of the timber and headed off in a straight line southeast across open brushy country toward Boundary Lake. With our yellow slickers we stood out as easy targets, but I didn't figure anyone who didn't know that country would be looking for us up there unless they just stumbled on us by air. Then even from a couple of thousand feet up we'd be dead easy to spot. We heard one chopper a ways off when we were just topping out, but it was too far off to see, so I figured nobody saw us. Lester wobbled a bit, and I hollered for him to pull up.

"You okay, bud?"

"I don't feel so good."

"Can you make it to the lake?"

"I don't know," he said.

"Another half hour?"

"Ain't it more like forty-five minutes, give or take?"

"Just breathe slow and deep and keep moving. There's no shelter here and no place to tie up."

"I won't let you down," he said.

"I know you won't."

He pushed the mare and led the way. He was riding slumped over now with nothing but hardheadedness holding him in the saddle. Ahead there was the trail, then beyond us the trees, and the lake beyond that with the peaks rising behind it. When we got closer to the lake, the trail forked. To the right a long meadow stretched off south at the top of a canyon. That trail led all the way down to Tuolumne Meadows and Tenaya Lake and into Yosemite Valley a couple of days' ride past that. Boundary Lake perched on the east border of the park, and we could see a peak called Crown Point rising beyond the water. We heard a plane coming from the south.

"Hey Lester, can you ride?"

"I thought I was," he said.

"I mean ride. Just slack your rein and hang on. We're making a run for those trees before we get spotted."

I goosed my horse into a half-assed trot, gigging him with my spurs as I dallied up, trying to drag that lead mule into a trot too. He finally broke into a lope, heaving himself forward at every stride with that full load on his back. The four behind him carrying the empty packs pulled back on their leads at first then got with the program too, some trotting, some loping. It was a mess, but that whole string came bouncing and clattering behind me. If the trees hadn't been close, I'd have lost the whole bunch soon enough. Harvey's mare busted into a long trot with Lester slumped forward just hanging on to his saddle horn. That old girl never liked anybody to get ahead of her, so Lester didn't have to ask her twice.

I pulled up when we were under enough tree cover to hide us. A small plane reared up way off past the lake for a second then disappeared behind Crown Point and the sound faded. I grabbed Lester's rein and pointed him back out toward the trail.

When we were closing in on the lake we hit some scattered timber and huge granite slabs. The trail wound through the granite and sometimes right over it when there was no place else to go. The horses and mules minded their footing on that bare rock, but Lester was as safe as anybody on that mare. Each animal took its sweet time, and nobody balked. We'd all been over it before.

We got to the west edge of Boundary Lake and kept on riding through the rocks to the north of the water. There were little campsites scattered all around the lake, but we had to find a good spot for the horses to graze and for a chopper to land. I hollered for Lester to pull up when we came to a place where the water was shallow and there was grass at the water's edge and trees for picket lines. This far into June we might have run across half a dozen camps around the lake, but all I saw was one red dome tent in some rocks on the south shore and no people anywhere. By then the rain had stopped again, and the sky was clearing.

I helped Lester off his horse and tied up the stock. I unpacked the mule with the bedrolls first and cleared a good spot for Lester to rest. When I'd unrolled his bed tarp, I walked him to it.

"Turn me thataway," he said.

"What the hell for?"

"I want to see Crown Point when I wake up."

"What's with you and Crown Point?"

He tapped the clasp of the watch. "Looks just like the Rolex logo," he said.

"You're a crazy bastard."

"Look." He held up his arm to show me.

"You're out of here tonight, bud. All you're going to see when you wake up is some ugly male nurse telling you to roll over so's he can stick a thermometer up your ass."

"At least I won't get rained on," he said.

"You know it never rains at night in the Sierra."

"Yeah, right."

I unbuckled the chinks from around his waist and steadied him so he could piss, and slid the Ruger off his belt so he wouldn't roll on it. I walked him back to his bedroll and laid him down. With the whisky and the shock he was probably dehydrated. I got him some water to drink then went back to unsaddling and hobbling the stock near the water's edge. They'd trash that grass pretty quick. Forest Service didn't like stock near the lake and backpackers would raise hell if there were any around, so once the chopper left I'd lead them down to the head of the meadow and hobble them out there for a time before I picketed them for the night.

When I saw Lester dozing I called Sarah again and told her where we'd camped.

"How's Les?"

"He'll live. Can we lift him out by dark?"

"I've got Tony Aguilar on the case," she said. "He's picking up a paramedic from Mammoth. They'll get Les stabilized then fly him to emergency there."

"Okay."

"I'll call you when he's in the air."

"Good."

"And Tommy?"

"Yeah?"

"I couldn't get hold of Nora Ross."

"I didn't figure you did."

There was still lots of daylight left. I checked on Lester, then set up picket lines between the trees a good ways from the lake so they'd be far from the helicopter when it landed. I started a fire where campers before us had set up a fire ring then scouted around for more wood. I had to circle wide to find enough. This was such a popular lake it had been picked clean over the years. I ended up catching my horse, throwing my saddle back on him, and riding him a ways from the lake to drag a hunk of deadfall limb into camp with my riata.

Lester had been watching me sort of half drowsy, but he had to laugh when I started to work on that log with a camp saw.

"Shouldn't have left the chain saw back at the forks, old scout," he said.

"You shouldn't have got yourself shot."

"Harvey's right," he said. "When we got to pack firewood into the high country, it's time to retire."

"You're twenty-six years old come October. You won't be retiring for two or three more years yet."

I got the fire going and set some water in a pan to boil next to the coffee pot. I poured some water for myself and washed down some aspirin with about a quart of it. When the pan was boiling I mixed Lester some instant oatmeal. He made a kid face when I brought it to him.

"That shit's nasty," he said.

"You need some food in you."

"Oughtta save it for the Boy Scouts."

"No time to cook you steak. You'll be in the air by dark."

I had him sit up and handed him the bowl, then I rocked him forward and checked on his bandage.

"How's she look?"

"It'll do till the paramedic gets here."

"Why don't you mix some Copenhagen with some mule shit like some sort of poultice?"

"What movie did you see that in?"

"No movie," he said. "Albert's Aunt Sally. Big medicine."

I yanked off the bandage and stuck on a new one. Other than bruising, the wound actually looked pretty good.

Nora's phone buzzed in my saddle pocket. Sarah told me that Tony and a paramedic were in the air. That gave me about forty-five minutes. An hour tops. I told Lester to get ready to travel. I caught up the stock and tied them to the picket lines good and snug. When they were all tied I fetched my rifle, poured myself some coffee, and sat on a rock next to Lester. He watched me slip the bolt, empty the magazine, and run a cleaning patch through the barrel, then reload and lock it down.

"You and that rifle," he said, laughing at me. "Are you riding down the switchbacks tonight?"

"Tomorrow."

"We rode down those suckers in the dark the day we climbed the Cleaver."

"We did a lot of stupid things up to and including now."

"But we had fun," he said.

"Well, since I won't have your expert help and since the switchbacks haven't been maintained since last time we rode 'em, I don't want to lead six head down in the dark."

"You could go back the way we came," he said.

"Where would the fun be in that?"

He scrunched around on his bedroll trying to get comfortable. I brought my rig close and stowed the .270 back in the scabbard, then took the Crown Royal out of the saddle pockets and poured some in my coffee.

"I'll take some of that," Lester said.

"Coffee'll just make you pee again. You don't want to mess Tony's upholstery." I handed him the bottle. "Here. With all you been drinking, another sip won't hurt you."

He took the bottle but just kind of looked at it.

"How much time do we have?" he asked.

"About thirty minutes. You gotta be someplace?"

"If we'd have come down twenty minutes later," he said, "they would have caught us out in the open in that cirque and we'd both be dead."

"Yeah."

"It all changes now, don't it."

"Uh-huh."

"We ought to get our stories straight."

"Just tell the truth, Lester."

He started counting on his fingers. "I got seven dead," he said. "Not counting Mister Billionaire."

"Seven?"

"Don't forget that Mexican girl they found below the dam," he said. "The one lured Albert to State Line."

"She was Cuban, I figure."

"So she makes seven."

He handed the whisky back without sipping any. I guess he'd had enough on the trail.

"That includes the two you shot today and the two drowned in the Escalade," he said.

"One of them didn't quite die."

"Okay, six."

"I'm glad you're keeping score."

"Can I ask you something?"

"No."

Chapter Fourteen

We could hear Tony's Jet Ranger before we could see it. We watched it from the time it was just a speck following the canyon up along the Tuolumne Meadows trail. It was traveling high, a couple of thousand feet or more, and sounded like an old-time movie projector. The shadows were long in the late afternoon, but even as high as we were there were no peaks close by to the west to hide the sun, just big pink and orange and blue clouds left over from the storm. When the chopper got over the lake, it bobbed and hovered like it was deciding where to light, and the sound bounced loud off the granite. I walked out on the grassy spot and waved it in.

I could see Tony Aguilar up in the cockpit with his earphones over that silver hair. He smiled down and nodded at us. A guy with a mustache and a uniform shirt sat behind him. I looked over at the picket line. One of the horses got a bit prancey, but after all the blowing up and shooting in the past twenty-four hours they were pretty solid. Lester put his hand on his hat and the surface of the lake quivered orange in the late sun as the chopper lowered itself with that lazy slap-slap-slap. It rocked to a stop on the grass by the water's edge, and the rotors slowed and stopped and it was quiet again.

The paramedic hopped out and lugged his bag over to Lester and started in on him. Tony stayed in the cockpit a minute, checking his instrument panel and switches and talking on his radio. He finally got out too. He wore a yellow inflatable survival vest I'd seen Navy pilots wear.

"How is he?" he asked.

"He'll be fine now. I'm glad as hell to see you."

"Give me a hand with the stretcher, my friend."

I followed him around the helicopter. He opened the double doors on the side and unbuckled a light evac stretcher with collapsible legs. I could see they had an IV bag already dangling from the ceiling with tubes hanging down and heart and respiration monitors ready to hook up.

"You done this before, pal."

Tony laughed. "Once or twice. Sarah prepped the paramedics by phone. You know Sarah."

"She's the best."

"Was it those Cubans shot him?"

"Yeah."

"I knew those bastards were trouble. What did you do to piss them off?"

"It's a long story."

"You tell it to me over a rib eye and a bottle of wine at the Sierra Peaks," he said.

"My treat."

We carried the stretcher over to Lester. The paramedic had him sitting up.

"You dress this?" he asked me. He was heavyset and wheezy from trotting in the high altitude.

"Yeah."

"Good job. Any idea what kind of round?"

"Probably five-point-seven high-penetration. Belgian."

He sort of whistled.

"Tommy," Tony said, "this is Mike Mildenburg from County. Lives down at McGee Creek."

"Hey, Mike."

"He's the EMT," Lester said. His words were already slurry.

"Paramedic," Mike said. He looked up at me. "I gave him some morphine."

"Morphine," Lester said. "Sweet. So what's the difference?"

"I can give you an IV, dress a gunshot wound, stuff like that," Mike said.

"He's the real deal, cowboy," Tony said. "We flown many rough miles together. He was in Desert Storm, weren't you, Mike."

Mike nodded at me. I nodded back.

"You got good veins," Mike said. "I see tourists so fat down in Mammoth you can't find a vein with a backhoe."

We made more small talk to keep Lester's brain occupied while Mike rooted around in the bullet hole and gave him a second shot of something. Then he slipped an IV needle into Lester's arm and started to tape it down. He worked fast.

"That's a cool vest." I said it like it was just something to say.

"Flight Commander-Two," Tony said. "These bad-boys don't come cheap."

"How's come you don't get one, Mike?" Lester asked.

"I'm a full-time county employee in a county full of freakin' cutbacks," he said. "They don't give a shit if I drown." He laughed. "But the Silver Fox here is a contractor."

"It's for the insurance," Tony said. "When they found out about all these lakes in this country, I got caught not wearing one and the bastards raised my rates."

"Way Tony flies," Mike said. "I'm more worried about the rocks than the water."

Lester tried to laugh, but he sounded nervous as hell. "When I was a kid, a contractor was the guy from Gardnerville who put in my dad's septic tank," he said.

"The word means something different now."

"The contractors carry guns where Tommy comes from," Tony said.

Mike looked up at my face where the splinters ripped it. "What happened to you?"

"I run into a door."

"Bullshit," Lester said. "I punched his lights out."

"Falling out among thieves?" Tony asked.

"You sound just like Sarah."

Tony sighed and put a hand on his chest. "Ah, my Sarah," he said, "*mi corazón*."

"Sarah with all them curves," Lester said, "and Tony with no brakes."

We all laughed.

"I'll give you something for it," Mike said. "You don't want it to get infected."

"I'm okay."

"Just the same," he said. "It hurt?"

"Like a bitch. I took some aspirin."

Mike finished taping off the IV needle, wrapping the tape completely around the arm to keep it rigid in case Lester thrashed around once he was airborne.

"Okay," he said. "He's ready."

He laid Lester down flat on his bedroll, and we set the stretcher down next to him and Mike showed us how to hoist him on without too much jostling.

"Do we set the legs down?" Tony asked.

"The ground's too rough," Mike said. "We'll have to just carry him."

"Mind you don't drop me," Lester said. "I'm a manly sonofabitch and I'm heavier than I look."

We got set and picked him up, Mike at the head, me at the feet, and Tony holding a side with one hand.

"Ay. You are most definitely heavier than you look," Tony said.

"Oh, how'd you know, you Argen-tine horn-dog?" Lester said. "You got the easy part."

When we got to the double doors without dropping him, the stretcher slid into place riding fore and aft. Mike strapped Lester down then set to work hooking up the IV and heart and respiration monitors. I walked back to Lester's bedroll to fetch his hat and phone. Hoisting Lester made my head throb like crazy, aspirin or not.

"He won't be wearing that for a couple of days," Mike said when I brought the hat.

"I ain't leaving without it," Lester said.

Mike handed me a tube of ointment. "It's an antibiotic and some aloe," he said. "It might keep your face from scarring."

"Tommy's scars don't show," Lester said. "Sarah says they're all on the inside."

"Bullshit." I set the phone on his belly, and he laid his hand over it, not really paying attention to it for once.

Mike climbed into the Ranger from the opposite side so he could reach the monitors from a rear jump seat. Tony walked down to the edge of the lake and just stood there looking out at the light from the late sun on the water like he was some nature boy.

"Well?" Lester said.

"You're on your way, bud. Clean sheets in about an hour."

"Everybody's going to a lot of trouble."

"It's no trouble."

"You coming down to Mammoth to see me?"

"Wouldn't miss it. But it'll be the middle of the day tomorrow before I even get off this mountain, and I'll have to call Sarah to have Harv meet me at Summers Lake with the stock truck."

"And a bottle of Jim Beam," he said.

"And a bottle of Jim Beam. You tell them to hold visiting hours till I get there."

"He's good to go," Mike said.

He waved at Tony. Tony trotted up from the lake around to our side of the chopper. He kept in good shape for an old bugger. It didn't bother him a bit to jog at ten thousand feet. It must have been the tennis.

"Are you ready, my friend?"

Lester nodded at Tony. He leaned in and tightened the straps over Lester's chest and legs good and snug.

"Don't want you falling out," he said. "Think of my insurance."

He climbed in to the pilot's seat and put on his headphones and checked his instruments. Mike buckled himself in the jumpseat next to Lester.

Lester just stared at the ceiling. "I let you down," he said just loud enough so I could hear. "I wouldn't listen to you, and I screwed up and let you down. This whole mess is my doing."

They had him strapped across the chest and legs and the right arm with the IV, but his left hand was free and I took it.

"You never let me down, Les."

Mike nodded it was time. I tousled Lester's head like a pup, then I pulled the double doors closed and checked the latches and stepped away. Tony fired up the motor, and I got a blast of wind from the rotors. I stepped back in a crouch from habit, hanging on to my hat, and snuck a look at the horses on the picketline to make sure I wouldn't be walking home in the dark. I could see Lester through the glass turning his head to watch me. Tony reached back to make sure I got the door good and tight and Lester stared up at the ceiling. Then Tony gave me a nod and a finger-point, revved up the motor, and lifted off. I took another couple of steps back and watched the Jet Ranger clear the ground and turn so it could pick up altitude over the lake away from the tall trees at the water's edge. There was that big roar and the wind blast and the swirl of pine needles and granite dust that drifted down when the chopper got above me, and the rippling the rotor wash made on the lake. I couldn't see Lester through the glare on the glass then, but Tony looked like he was rising out of his seat all of a sudden. I tried to see, and figured he maybe had just inflated his vest. I could sort of make out Mike leaning forward like he was saying something, then the chopper turned and rose straight up over the water, the noise from the motor reverbing off the mountainsides. When I could see sky under the chopper's belly, there wasn't anything left for me to do. Lester was safe now and on his way. I turned to check on the horses.

Then the noise stopped. I whipped around to look. The blades kept spinning, but there was no sound from the motor, only the cut of the blades in the thin air. The Ranger rose an instant more, then just stopped in the sky, hanging there about a hundred feet over the water with the motor dead. Then, with the rotors still whipping around slow, the helicopter fell like the bottom had been pulled out from under it. It fell for two or three seconds with the rotors slowing it down and Tony wrestling with the controls, but it seemed like forever. Then it splashed into the lake about two hundred yards out. I ran to the bank. The lake was only maybe forty feet away from me, but when I got to the water's edge the chopper was already halfway under. It had stayed upright when it fell, but it rolled to the side as soon as it hit with one blade pointing up, a second one almost under water. A cockpit door was open, so water was pouring in, and I could see at least one of them scrambling to get out as the chopper sunk deeper. I was yelling Lester's name. I could see a squirt of steam as the icy water hit the motor. Then the whole thing went under and was gone. Just like that. The flat water bubbled when a big pocket of air popped up, but all that meant was there was nothing left to breathe inside. It didn't matter. The water was so cold from the snowmelt that even with air anyone inside would die of hypothermia in a few minutes, and anyone trying to swim halfway across the lake would go the same way. I stood knee-deep in the lake, just panting like I wanted to puke. I could barely see a little spot of yellow bobbing on the water moving toward the opposite shore. Tony must have got out alive.

I slogged out of the lake not even remembering throwing my hat and jacket on the ground and wading in. I picked them up and headed for our campfire. I rolled my dad's saddle over and pulled his .270 out of the scabbard and walked back to the lake. I lay across a big slab of granite and put the scope on the little yellow spot. Through the lens I could make out Tony swimming a few strokes with an overhand crawl, then he paused like he was tiring out and treading water, and it looked like he might sink, slipping right out of the survival vest. The vest was inflated for sure now. He started swimming again, more like a breast stroke to save his strength. If he didn't reach the opposite shore pretty soon, the cold would get him too. Even with the scope, all I could see was the back of his white head over that yellow vest. I swung the barrel of the rifle back on the spot on the water where the chopper had gone down to see if there was any movement. The orange of the sunset had gone and the surface of the lake was smooth and gray. I guessed the water was maybe forty to fifty feet deep out there. Freezing and black. If Lester was alive he'd have lost consciousness. That was about all I could hope for. Strapped down like he was, he never had a chance.

I swung the barrel back. Through the scope I picked up Tony crawling out of the water on his hands and knees through the rocks. He was close to the campsite with the dome tent. I could see him stopped on the bank on all fours like he was catching his breath, then he got up and sort of staggered to that tent. When he got there, he dropped to his knees again and looked like he was scouting around inside. When he finally got up, he had wrapped himself in something, either a blanket or a sleeping bag. It was hard to tell through the scope, and Tony was moving all the time to warm himself up. Then I saw that he was waving his arms and gesturing like he was talking, and I traced him with the crosshairs. When he stopped moving for a second, I saw he was talking on a phone. I held the rifle dead steady on the rock to get a good look. I saw him gesture some more. Then with the reticle laid right on him, he pointed across the lake nodding his head toward our camp and sort of smiled. He looked real relieved. That's when I blew his head off.

I kept the scope on him as he dropped. He tumbled backwards, and when his upper body hit the rocks in that inflated vest he looked like he almost bounced. I walked back to my saddle and got the cartridge box and stuffed it in my pocket. If there was one more accident left to happen, then I'd be it. It took me about fifteen minutes to walk around the east edge of the lake to the south shore where I'd dropped Tony. Most of the way I was on the old packer trail, but part of the route I had to climb big rocks and push through whitebark and hemlock thickets, keeping my eye on that dome tent while looking back at my camp now and again.

I kept the .270 on the tent when I got to the campsite. There was enough flat ground next to it for a chopper to have landed. I stepped around Tony and squatted down to look inside. There was a car-camper's sleeping bag, lots of food, a bottle of Johnny Walker Black Label, and an AK-47. All a tad too heavy for backpacking. Part of the dome drooped where the frame hadn't been put together right, and the whole thing hadn't been pegged down like it had been set up in a hurry. I walked back to Tony. He still held the satellite phone in his fist. I picked it up and listened. I could hear salsa music. I waited a bit more.

"*Buenas tardes, Teófilo.*"

"Tony?" the voice on the phone said. The voice was real deep and rumbly.

"Tony's dead."

It was quiet for a minute. Even the music got quiet.

"Did you kill him, soldier?"

"With pleasure. And I'm going to kill you too if I get the chance, Señor Pozolero."

I could hear him laugh. "You won't come close, asshole," he said. "You wouldn't even know where to start."

"That was a smart trick, cutting off the motor for a controlled drop."

"That Tony is a good pilot," he said.

"Almost as good as GQ."

"You're too smart for your own good, soldier. I hope your night on that lonely mountain passes without incident. After grieving for your friend drowned in the freak helicopter accident, it was a shame that you ran down the trail and fell off the steep cliff. They may not find your body for such a long time."

"Yeah. Like anybody'd believe I'd run when I could ride. And you're forgetting about Tony's body."

"Bodies vanish, asshole," he said, "remember?"

I set the phone next to Tony without punching off. Then I searched him. He had a lot of cash in his wallet but that was normal for him. He always liked flashing a roll. The wallet was soaked and I stuffed it back in his pocket. He had a Glock in a holster on his belt. That would have been to use on me if he'd needed to. I racked the slide, wiped it off and put it in his hand. I didn't figure on spending a single night in jail for killing that prick. I took the AK-47 from the tent, popped the steel clip and threw it out into the lake, and heaved the Kalashnikov in after it with both hands. Then I walked back around the lake to our camp to hobble the horses and mules with the last of the grain before I picketed them for the night. Nora's phone started buzzing after a while. That would be Sarah, but I didn't know what to say and I didn't want her up here with me until the last shoe dropped. I didn't think I could even talk yet anyway.

I laid the whole log across the fire and tended the stock. When I was finished, the log was blazing right along. I poured myself a drink and stared at the flames. I ate a couple of pudding cups I'd packed for Lester, just to soak up the whisky in my stomach. Besides, the sugar would jack me up. When the log had burned partway through, I lifted the end and banged it around in a big cloud of sparks until it broke at the burned place. I stacked the two chunks together and the fire really got going. By dark the flames were as tall as I was, popping with sparks shooting way up in the sky. The firelight showed high up in the tamarack circling the camp like I was inside a teepee of orange flame moving around me in the branches. It let me see everything, the horses on the picket line, Lester's bedroll, our packs and saddles, and sent a shimmer of flame out on the water all the way across the lake.

I left Lester's bedroll where it was and unrolled mine close by. I checked the cylinder of his Ruger and stuffed it in my jacket pocket. Then I took my rifle, the whisky bottle, and a couple of saddle blankets and climbed into the rocks above the picket line to wait. It was another half hour before they showed. The first sign was a little flashlight flicker way across the lake where I'd left Tony's body. The flicker went dark fast, and it took them forever to circle the lake. Flatlanders. As usual there was a pair of them. When they finally showed they moved toward the bedrolls, each of them carrying a chunk of tree limb, creeping at the edge of the firelight like cavemen. When they saw nobody was in the bedrolls, they looked around at the jumping shadows in the dark. It would be another fifteen minutes before moonrise. The stock was quiet on the picket line. These were two spooked city boys on a big empty black mountain, dressed for a warm June evening, not ten thousand feet.

"*Holá*, scumbags. *Qué tal?*"

They looked around when I hollered, dropping their clubs and raising their guns, ready to shoot but not seeing a thing to shoot at. Just the dark and the fire. It would have been easy to drop them both, but I didn't want bodies in camp that night, and I didn't want to perturb the stock. When they figured that they wouldn't be beating me to death and dumping my corpse down the switchbacks and couldn't see any advantage in playing sitting duck, they backed out of the firelight and beat it. I could see the flashlight glow as they hustled back around the lake. The light disappeared in the rocks and trees heading for the Summers Lake Trail. I slipped down toward the lake outside of the firelight, keeping my eye on where I'd last seen their flash. When I got to the water, I fired half the cylinder of the Ruger across the lake in the general direction of the dome tent. I didn't want them going back to mess with Tony's body, and that .357 made plenty of noise. It would be those boys walking down the switchbacks in the dark tonight, not me. I waited a bit before I climbed back to my spot in the rocks.

I sat up there for a long time wrapped in that saddle blanket with my rifle. Finally I was ready and called Sarah.

She said she was just lifting off from the Piute Meadows airstrip in the Highway Patrol helicopter.

"They are going out of their minds in Mammoth," she said, "so I was coming to look for you. I was afraid something happened to Les."

"Lester's dead, Sarah."

She made a sound then was still for a minute. "You said he—"

"The chopper crashed into the lake on takeoff. Tony crashed it on purpose. Lester and the paramedic drowned right in front of me."

She tried to say something like oh god but just made a sobbing, gurgling noise, then the phone was quiet. She'd known Lester his whole life, just like me. She started to say my name, then ask how, but the words wouldn't come out.

"It was planned. Tony planned it. Some controlled drop thing they teach chopper pilots for emergencies. Tony swam away, but Lester was strapped in. The paramedic was trapped in the back." I stopped. I couldn't talk any more either.

She was quiet for another minute. When she finally could talk she was all business.

"But why?"

"Same reason they drove Callie off the road."

I heard her take a deep breath.

"Put Tony on the phone."

"Tony's dead."

"But you said he . . . I see. Good."

"You'll want to have Mitch send whoever's on duty to the Summers Lake campgrounds and wait just above

229

the trailhead with lights off for a couple of ATV's or two Cubans on foot coming in from Boundary Lake. They got automatic weapons, so your guys best look sharp."

"I'll call right now," she said. "You sit tight. I'll be up there in thirty minutes."

She clicked off. There wasn't any point in arguing with her. By then the moon had rose up just past full, so she could guide the pilot by sight following the canyon trail up from the campgrounds and making the turn at Henry Lake, staying high enough to avoid the peaks. They'd see my campfire easy enough, but I lit the Colemans and set them out on either side of the patch of grass so they'd know where to land. No one likes flying those things at night if they can help it. You got to be nuts. I could hear the Highway Patrol chopper thumping up the canyon from down by Henry Lake and see the searchlight before they cleared the rim. It flew in with the running lights flashing and the moon behind it and set down right where Tony had.

Sarah climbed out slow, looking around. The pilot was a guy I didn't know. Sarah wore her ranch clothes and hat instead of her uniform, but she had her service belt with the 9mm strapped on, her nylon deputy coat, and carried the 12 gauge pump out of her cruiser. I could tell she'd been crying, but so had I. She gasped a bit when she saw my face, which probably looked like hell in the firelight. She set the shotgun down and just held me for a minute, and the only sound was the chatter of the radio on her belt and the whap-whap of the chopper idling. When she pulled back, she put her fingers on the raw spots on my cheek but didn't say anything. Then she walked back to the helicopter and talked to the pilot. He nodded and she stepped back, and the chopper revved up and lifted off. We watched it fly east into the moon then disappear down over the rim.

"You staying?"

"He's sending a CHP black-and-white to the campground to back up our guys," she said. She took a big breath. "Show me?"

She picked up the 12 gauge and followed me back to the lake. She took the Maglite from her belt, but turned it off when I asked her to. It would be easier to follow the trail in the moonlight and wouldn't draw attention. I pointed to her belt and shook my head and she turned off the radio, too. First I showed her where the Jet Ranger took off, and pointed out to the spot where it sunk.

"He must have been so scared," she said. I could barely hear her.

We circled the lake like I'd done before. I stayed watchful toward the trail ahead in case those last two shooters had changed their minds about walking home. When we got around to the other side, I showed her Tony's body. It was just like I left it, so the Cubans hadn't messed with him. She looked at him for a minute in the moonlight then turned her flash on him. I could see her sort of wince when she saw that the back of his head was gone.

"Does it usually happen that way?"

"If you do it right."

She ran the beam over the Glock in his fist, then over the inflated vest.

"Did he try to shoot you?"

"No. I was clear across the lake."

She just nodded. "He looks huge," she said.

"It's the vest."

"It looks like you shot the Michelin man."

"I knew something was hinkey when he inflated it just after takeoff. I never figured on this."

"How could he kill two men he'd known for years with no more thought than . . ." she said. The words came out hard. "Mike Mildenberg has a wife and a seven-year-old."

"They'd have killed Tony quick enough if he hadn't."

"Like that's an excuse," she said.

"He'd been working for GQ before today. He's my pick for the one who snatched the body from the plane last week. And the one told GQ that Albert would make a likely patsy."

"Oh god, poor Les," she said. "Tony was always the one I'd call. Everybody knew that."

I showed her the tent to keep her busy. She turned on her flashlight again and poked at stuff but didn't touch anything. I showed her how it was just thrown up more like a prop than a shelter. I told her about the Kalashnikov I tossed into the lake.

"You might have wanted to leave it for evidence," she said.

"I left you the Glock. That AK's the bad-guy weapon of choice. I didn't come home eleven thousand miles to get shot by one. You want a Kalashnikov, I left one with a couple more bodies back at the forks."

She gave me a real strange look.

"The two that shot Lester?"

232

"Yeah."

We walked back to Tony's body. She ran her light over his face for a minute without saying anything.

"I never went to bed with him," she said, "if that's what you're thinking."

"Never said you did."

"But you thought it. You and Les and everybody."

"Nope. I figured he wasn't your type."

"There was a time he was exactly my type," she said.

She turned off the flashlight, and I let her lead the way back along the trail to our camp. My fire still reflected across the lake. When we were close to where the trail forked off toward the switchbacks, a branch rustled out ahead of us and we both froze. I motioned for her to stay still and stepped ahead of her. She moved the shotgun muzzle to the side and I waited two or three minutes with my rifle ready, but there was no other sound.

"Probably just an owl or marmot or something."

"Or a bear," she said.

"You sound exactly like Lester." It just came out like that before I even thought.

When we got into the camp, she set the shotgun down and sat on a rock, huddled in her jacket.

"Think you've got enough wood on that fire?"

"I didn't want you to get lost."

She got up and stood by the fire, then turned her back to it and stared out at the lake. When she couldn't stand it anymore, she watched me slip the .270 back into the scabbard.

"Is that a nightscope?"

"Nope." We both kind of glared at each other. "Didn't think I'd be needing one."

"I'm sorry," she said. "I just . . . I don't know. I just can't believe all this is happening."

"I know."

She watched me unlace my packers and take off my wet socks. I set the boots close to the fire and got dry socks from my bedroll.

"Where do all these people come from?"

"Who knows. Cuba, Miami, Sinaloa, Hell."

"How many more, do you think?"

"Millions."

She sat back down on the rock.

"I hope you don't mind my, I don't know. My being here," she said. "I didn't want you to be alone."

"I know."

"And I don't want to be alone."

That was exactly what Nora Ross had said. "I'm glad you're here."

"Are we safe here?"

"No. I don't know. Safe as anyplace. I feel better up here anyway."

"Shows what you know," she said, but she smiled kind of sad when she said it.

I dug out some cheese and crackers. When I held up the Crown Royal bottle she nodded, and I poured her some in a Sierra cup. She moved over and sat on the rock next to me and went back to staring at the fire. She was always the hardnose about doing the right thing and following the straight and narrow and all that. Especially since she became a deputy. Now she just sat there and tried not to cry. After a while I put my boots back on, got up, and took my rifle and checked the stock on the picket line. When I was finished, I walked the perimeter just outside the firelight. I could hear her radio then, and hear her talking to someone. When I got back, the moon was way up and she was taking off her boots and jacket and crawling into my bedroll by the fire. A toothbrush stuck out of her shirt pocket, her radio was off, and the 12 gauge lay on the ground between two saddle pads to keep the dew off the bluing but close enough for her to grab.

"I called in," she said. "I told them we had a crime scene, but it was secure till morning. It would be too risky to send another chopper out at night."

"Okay."

"I told them you could show them everything tomorrow." She looked up at me from the bedroll. "Do you mind?"

"No, but you'd have more room in Lester's bed."

She pushed her socks and toothbrush under the fold of the canvas and scrunched over so I'd have some space.

"I couldn't," she said. "I'd cry all night."

I crawled into the bedroll next to her and she put her arm over me like we did this all the time. I must have stiffened up.

"Come on," she said. "Move over. It's not like you haven't thought of this before." She tried to laugh but started to sob.

I held her then and kissed where the hair grows soft just past the corner of your eye. She held me close, front to front, and kissed me on the raw cheek, her tears getting it wet and stinging until she'd wore herself out and stopped crying. She'd pecked me on the cheek a million times and given me big sister hugs, but laying this close felt different and I didn't fight it much. She made a little sound like she wasn't fighting it much either.

"If Lester could see us," she said, "he'd laugh his head off."

She could barely get the words out, but when she did, I was the one who just lost it.

Chapter Fifteen

I tried to stay awake. I'd figured to slip out and spend the night wrapped in a saddle blanket with my rifle up above the picket lines, watching from the dark, but I passed out and slept till sunup for the second straight day. Sarah was still holding me when I woke up. She looked wrecked.

"You finally slept," she said.

We crawled out of the bedroll and tended to the stock, leading them to water two at a time then hobbling them out to graze. There wasn't much feed left, but we'd be out of there quick enough. I got a breakfast fire going from the last night's embers, and we rolled up the beds while we waited for the coffee to boil. I handed Sarah a cup then took her hand and led her down to the lake. I left my rifle and the shotgun behind, but I still had Lester's Ruger reloaded and in my jacket pocket. We walked around the lake, and when we got to Tony's body I started climbing up in the rocks and through the snow and she followed. We got up a ways then we stopped and turned around, looking down on the dome tent and across the lake to the horses and mules at the edge of camp. Then we climbed a little higher. When we looked down again we could see the Jet Ranger in the clear water, the rotors only down about twenty feet. Once our eyes adjusted we could see it all. I would have thought the lake was deeper there. If it had been ten minutes later, the morning sun reflecting on the surface would have hid it. It sat upright with the one door open and the rotors intact like it could fly right out of there. Neither one of us said a word. We just held hands and stared down at it. After a minute we walked back to grab some breakfast before we saddled up.

Sarah cooked sausage and eggs on the fire, taking her time while I mantied up our goods, dividing the camp stuff into light loads for two animals, not just the one mule who'd carried it all before.

Then we ate and I told her everything. About how we found the plane that morning fixing trail seven days before, how it looked, and how Lester swiped the watch and money from the body so we didn't dare report it to her office that first night. I told her how Callie got dollar signs in her eyes, and how she and Lester started stirring the pot right off, calling GQ and the wife's lawyers from the cabin, trying to make something happen. I told her how the wreck had been tampered with when we got back two days later, the body gone and the fake note left behind, and how spooked we were when we knew we'd started something we couldn't finish. She pretty much knew the rest, about Callie, about Albert, about the jacket planted in Albert's Firebird, and the Cuban hottie who got killed because she was probably just somebody's junkie whore who couldn't be trusted to keep her mouth shut. I told her about meeting Nora in the cabin by the lake, and how we had to hide and just got out before the Cubans blew it up. I left out the part in the Ponderosa Motel, but Nora had said women always know anyway. And finally, I told her how GQ figured he'd pretend to discover the wreck and claim his dad had walked away, and how the only way for that story to stick was for Lester and me and anyone who knew the truth to be dead.

"Is that why you didn't tell me," she asked, "to protect me?"

"No. I was just too chicken to tell you the mess I made."

"You're not chicken. Wound a little tight, but never chicken."

"I figured if there wasn't any wreck, GQ's whole story would look like a lie."

"Good guess," she said. "The Reno news crew said their chopper couldn't find the plane where he said it was. It started to sound like a scam."

"When was this?"

"Yesterday afternoon," she said.

"We heard a chopper, but I couldn't tell where it was heading."

"There's one thing you still haven't told me."

"What?"

"Where's the plane?"

"Everywhere. It's hid in pieces from North Pass to the Forks to Aspen Pass. Every-damn-where."

"You're totally crazy," she said.

Her county radio chattered and she picked it up.

"Give me a minute," she said. "I've got to give Mitch the Cliff Notes version."

I started cleaning up the plates while she talked into the radio.

"Hey Mitch. Yeah, I'm still up here at Boundary Lake with Tommy Smith. Right. I flew up with CHP last night. Here's what I know. Les Wendover and Mike Mildenberg were murdered by Tony Aguilar. He tried to make it look like a chopper accident, but Tommy figured it out. Then Tony tried to shoot Tommy and Tommy shot him in self-defense. No. Tony was working for the same people who killed Callie Dean and Albert Coffey. No, not Mexicans. Cubans from Miami and the missing guy's son. Big money."

She looked up at me for a minute, listening.

"No. The meth was bogus. To throw us off the track, of course. Callie was trying to work some sort of con on the son and his family. Get them fighting, saying she knew where his father's plane crashed, trying to get paid for her information." She listened some more. "I told you, there was no meth. Callie stumbled on a scheme by the son to defraud the estate. Right, huge, huge money. That made her a target, then Les too. What do you mean how do I know there was no meth? God, Mitch, concentrate. I know these people." Without looking my way she reached her hand out to take mine. That surprised the hell out of me. She kept on, talking about GQ getting Tony to make drowning Lester look accidental, and how much he must have paid him, about the Cubans at the bridge and the two more at the forks. She told him we were only up there fixing trail. Then she let go of my hand and got one of her cross looks.

"My god, Mitch. These guys had automatic weapons. Tommy only had an old deer rifle. Yes, he *is* that good. And lucky for him."

She nodded a couple of more times. "Can you get hold of Harvey Linderman and have him meet us at the Summers Lake campground with his stock truck between noon and one?" She listened another minute. "No, Tommy can't wait. He's got seven head he's got to get off this mountain. He can give us a flyover later." She listened some more, then said yeah and switched off.

"Well that's a flat pack of lies, Sarah."

"It's half of the truth," she said.

"Yeah. You left out the half with the plane, is all."

"I just bought you a day to figure a way to tell the other half and not go to jail or get yourself in a tangle with lawyers. It's either that or we pick up every piece of the wreck and I watch you spend a month putting it all back together."

"I got to make this right."

"I know you do."

"Starting with Mitch."

"Mitch is an idiot," she said.

I finished washing the plates and we went to saddling up. We worked without talking like we had been doing this together for years. She caught me watching her cinch up one of the mules.

"I've worked cattle with you and rode in the Fourth of July parade and we've team roped," she said, "but this is new."

"Yeah?"

"It's kind of okay."

"You should go to work for Harvey."

"Yeah, right. Think of the career opportunities."

Working together, we got the two light loads up and tarped and lashed down good and tight with me taking the lead on the hitches. I'd saddled my horse with Lester's rig for her to ride, and I went to hand him to her. She was cradling the 12 gauge in her arm.

"How you going to carry that thing down the switchbacks and lead a string of mules too?"

"You tell me," she said. "You're the packer."

I took it from her, shucked the shells then wrapped it in her jacket and tied it longwise along the top of the sawbuck on an unloaded mule.

"What else did Mitch say?"

"That he was sorry," she said. "Sorry for all of us."

"He didn't sound sorry. He sounded pissed."

"He said he and two Highway Patrol officers picked up a Cuban with an assault rifle at the trailhead around midnight. The jerk came bouncing into the campground on an ATV with the light on. They'd been watching him come down the trail for half a mile. A kid could have caught him. Mitch has him in custody, but he's not talking. *No habla inglés.* He was pretty thrashed after his little hike down the switchbacks, and real afraid."

"He should be. Just one guy?"

"Just one," she said. "The other must have been smarter and slipped by in the dark."

"That leaves at least two of them still loose."

I put the shells in a ziplock and tossed them in an empty pack bag.

"Hop on and check your stirrups. Lester's legs are probably longer than yours."

She swung up. "Shows how observant you've been all these years," she said. "They're fine."

"That's 'cause he rides with 'em shorter than you." I handed her the roan with a mule tied behind. "I'll go first on Harvey's mare. She hates being in the back, but she's real good on the gnarly spots." The stirrups still looked too long for her, but I didn't say another word.

I checked my cinch, stepped aboard, and untied the big black packhorse. When I led him and two mules past Sarah, she was staring at the lake. She had her sunglasses on so I couldn't see her red eyes.

"I don't ever want to come back here," she said.

I pulled up and looked out at the lake. It was a nice clear day with the sun hitting the snow on Crown Point and the peak reflecting on the water.

"You got to. You can't blame the place."

"Tommy, that first night when you knew that Les had stolen the watch from the wreck, why didn't you just call me and tell me about it? You could have said he took it as proof of identity or something. The money might've been a problem, but anything would have been better than this."

"I guess I got the rest of my life to come up with an answer to that." I led the way out of the trees to the trail around the lake.

We were spread out single file, so we didn't talk once we left the lake and started down the switchbacks. Some of the backcountry trails were deer trails, stock trails, or Indian paths over the mountains as old as time, but this trail was picked and shoveled and dynamited by packers, the Forest Service, and the CCC over the last hundred years. When the old Summers Lake pack outfit went under, the Forest Service didn't waste any more time maintaining it. The switchbacks would be good enough for backpackers if they were tough enough, but there were some real dicey spots for stock, so Harvey and horse campers hadn't used it for years. As hairy as that trail was, the clear sky gave us long views of the country below us and a high-up look right into the snowy granite peaks just to the south. I felt damn near close enough to touch the one that Lester had never stopped talking about since that day we climbed it in cowboy boots when we were seventeen.

I got off a couple of times and led my string real slow over some slides where there were boulders on the trail and nasty drop-offs and no way around but over. The pack horses and mules were pros, and since only two of the five carried a load, they could concentrate on their footing. When I'd get past a bad spot, I'd wait for Sarah to do the same before I got mounted, but she was hand enough I didn't worry about her.

When we got partway down the switchbacks, we looked down into a cirque with a meadow and trees at the near end of it, and Henry Lake at the far end off to the north. The switchbacks cut across the face of the rock above the meadow. At the furthest end of the lake there was a stand of tamarack and a stretch of beach. The water there was shallow and looked yellow over the sand. I was looking out at the lake when I saw the ravens. There was a cluster of them down at the bottom of the switchbacks. When I looked out, I saw a few more cruising the thermals and a single turkey vulture circling above them like he was figuring if whatever was down there was worth tangling with that bunch. Then the buzzard hit a downdraft and flapped those long wings, fighting to get himself some altitude. I pulled up and turned in the saddle to get Sarah's attention, but she'd already seen it. She pointed to the rocks and brush down below.

"I guess that's why Mitch only caught the one," she yelled.

I nodded and we kept on riding. When we got closer to the meadow we could see the body. We crossed a worn-away spot, a hole in the trail where backpackers had cut the switchback and made a slide, a kind of chute between the two parallel legs of the trail, one about ten feet above the other. Hikers thought it was fun to skitter down a cut-off like that, but they made it dangerous for stock. The second Cuban must have hit that slide in the moonlight and lost his footing. The drop to the meadow was only about sixty feet, but he probably bounced off some nasty hunks of granite on the way down. The animals picked their way over the worn-away spot, and we kept on going to the end of the switchback and reversed direction again.

"Should we check to see if he's still alive," Sarah said, "or do we take the ravens' word for it?"

"The ravens. Those two Cubans were definitely the C-Team."

Within a few minutes we were riding along the edge of the meadow on the floor of the cirque with mountains on three sides and the lake ahead of us and only five miles to go to the trailhead. We came on the second ATV below Henry Lake. The Cubans had ridden up as far as they could until the trail got rocky, then left the ATV right in plain sight. I got off and looked at the sticker on the gas tank.

"It's from a rental outfit in Mammoth." I jotted the name in my tallybook.

"Why would they be down in Mammoth?" she asked.

We made such good time once we got down into the canyon in the sagebrush that we beat Harvey to the trailhead by half an hour.

He drove up in the stock truck. Dave Cathcart followed in his pickup. They parked under the Jeffrey pines by what was left of the corrals and outhouse of the old pack outfit. We shook hands all around and Sarah hugged her dad for a minute, but nobody hardly said a word. Harvey and May had been just crazy about Lester like he was their own son. We stripped the packs and saddles and loaded them in the bed of Dave's truck. The first thing I untied was Sarah's shotgun and handed it to her. We stopped when two more cars drove up from the campgrounds. One was a county sheriff's SUV, the second was a sedan that said U.S. Marines. Mitch got out, nodded at the rest of us, and took Sarah off past the outhouse to talk. A major in woodland camo got out of the car carrying a binder.

"Sergeant Smith?" he asked.

I walked over and we shook. He wasn't much older than me, head shaved under his cap and with a long burn scar on his forearm that went up under his short sleeve and showed on the side of his neck. He said his name was Tuggle, and he was the Sea Stallion pilot from the training base who'd be hauling the Jet Ranger out of Boundary Lake as soon as they flew in a SEAL crew to rig things up. He opened the binder. It was full of laminated topo maps. He'd flown over the lake before and knew the spot where I showed him to land, and knew the section of the lake where the chopper went down. I told him the depth, the type of helicopter, and the best place to put a diving crew in the water.

"You're welcome to fly with us," he said.

"I'll go if you need me, but I'd rather not."

"I understand, Sergeant."

He was probably the only one who did.

"I'd take it as a favor if you didn't ask Deputy Cathcart either. She'd feel like it was her duty, but it would be real hard on her."

"Consider it done," he said.

We shook again, and he walked over and said something to Mitch, then he got in his car and drove back toward the campgrounds.

Dave and Harvey and I finished loading the stock, and we all waited for Mitch to finish with Sarah. After a bit the two of them walked back. Mitch carried the 12 gauge.

"What's this bullcrap about another body at Henry Lake?" he said.

I started walking over to the stock truck.

He followed me. "You'll need to come by and make a statement."

"I'll be by soon as I get these animals squared away." I walked back to Dave's pickup and rooted around in one of the pack bags in the bed.

"Don't keep us waiting," Mitch said. "You got this county shot up like Tijuana on a Saturday night. No doubt about it. I'm just glad your dad isn't alive to see it."

I pulled the ziplock with the 12 gauge shells out of the bag and tossed them at him.

"Catch."

He took a grab but missed, and the ziplock landed in the pine duff. I walked over to the stock truck and climbed in the cab and slammed the door. When I looked back, Mitch was getting into his SUV. Harvey climbed up behind the wheel next to me and fired up the GMC.

"I'm real sorry about that little mule, Harv."

He kind of grunted but couldn't say anything just then. He reached into his shirt and pulled out a half pint of Jim Beam. I took it and had a pull, then another, then handed it back. He had a pull and buried it back in his shirt. I watched Sarah through the windshield picking up the ziplock and getting in her dad's pickup. She didn't look back. After they all drove away, their dust hung like fog under the pines.

Chapter Sixteen

We ran the stock down the loading chute, and I popped open a bale of hay and spread it in the mangers along the corral fence. The saddle horses left out in the meadow ran up to get a share. We pulled the saddles and packs from Dave's pickup and stowed them in the shed.

"Don't suppose anyone's called Lester's folks."

"Mitch had a deputy from up there tell them Lester was killed, no more'n that," Harvey said. "May was going to call, but she hadn't stopped crying. I can if you'd rather."

"No. I'll drive over to Grass Valley tomorrow."

"They'd like that," Sarah said, "I'll go with you if you want." Her nose and eyes were red, and she sounded stuffed up.

"You wouldn't want to piss off Mitch."

"Old Mitch looked like he'd been weaned on a pickle back there at the campground," her dad said.

"Mitch and Tommy have a history," Sarah said. "A real unfortunate history."

"We was just like brothers till he pulled me over one night out by the reservoir when I was sixteen and slammed me face-down on the hood of my mom's Camaro. Anybody want a beer?"

"Hell yes," Harvey said.

"Let's see if those damn Cubans left us any Coors." I got up and walked to the trailer. I wanted to do this while the sun was up and folks were around. Inside, it was the same beechwood veneer on the walls and the bench seat under the front window where I always bunked, the same fishing rods hanging on the rack behind the door, the same Forest Service poster—a Charley Russell painting of a horse bucking through a cookfire—with the big letters along the top saying Prevent Range Fires. The same sink and fridge and the oven-door glass all brown from smoke and grease, and the narrow hall heading back to the shower and toilet and bedroom, and the same kerosene lamps on the table. And Lester's crap just about everywhere, even the bag of chocolate chip cookies he'd left on the counter.

I brought the beer out and we all sat on the pack platforms under the aspens, but I couldn't sit still.

"Come on, Dave. Let's take a look at your colt."

He got up and followed me down to the corral. The colt looked up as I walked over to where he was munching hay at the manger between a couple of the mules. I slipped a hackamore on him and led him out.

"He's coming along real nice." I hobbled the colt in the shade, talking to him and rubbing him down.

"I can see that," he said. "I'm surprised you had any time for him."

"I wanted to get him going for you."

"He let you trim his feet?" he asked.

"After I roped a foot or two. Messed with 'em."

"You got on him yet?"

"Yeap. But I put in a lot of groundwork first so's he'll be rock solid. You know, for an older gentleman such as yourself."

He laughed at that. "Oh, he's not for me." He looked over at Sarah. She was walking up the trailer step to go inside. "You putting a start on him will be icing on the cake for her. But don't say anything. It's a surprise."

"You got it."

I saddled him up and led him around, and he was as good as could be. I had used my dad's rig once I unbuckled the rifle scabbard. I knew Dave would recognize it. Then I hobbled him again so he could just stand quiet for a while.

Sarah came out of the trailer ten minutes later with a towel around her neck. She was dressed, but her hair was wet and she was wearing one of my shirts.

"You mind?" she asked. "I just had to shower."

I sort of shrugged.

"Dad," she said, "we better get going."

"Okay, doll," he said.

"Are you coming, Tommy?"

"I thought I'd clean up first."

"Okay," she said. "I'll wait for you in town. We'll see Mitch together if you want."

"Yeah."

"That is sure a nice colt, Dad."

I said so long to Dave and Harvey and unsaddled the colt and turned him back into the corral as they drove off. I picked up my jacket and Lester's chinks, slid my rifle out of the scabbard and went into the trailer. I got myself a glass of water and sat at the table. I pulled Nora's satellite phone out of the jacket pocket and called Grass Valley. When I was done talking to Lester's dad, I drank the rest of the water and left the phone on the table and stood at the sink for a minute. Then I hung the chinks on a wall hook, stood the rifle in the closet, and went into the back to shower. The stall was warm and steamy from Sarah just using it, and the soap was still wet.

I took my time straightening up the place. Finally I sat down again with a yellow pad and wrote out a time line of everything that happened since that morning I first saw the wreck, checking my tallybook now and again. It was harder to write than I thought. When I tore it out of the pad I had four pages. I folded them up and put them in one of Lester's old finance company envelopes.

I picked up the satellite phone again and punched Nora's cell number. I kind of jumped when I heard a female voice say yes.

"Damn it, woman, where have you been? Are you alright?"

I heard a kind of gasp.

"Nora?"

"No, Tommy," she said. It was Sarah.

I didn't say anything for a minute.

"She's dead, isn't she."

"How did you know?" Sarah asked.

"You wouldn't have answered her phone otherwise."

"Oh god, Tommy."

"Where are you?"

"The Ponderosa Motel," she said. "It's pretty bad. Gerald Q is here, too."

"Well, that's something."

"Are you coming down? You sound awful."

"Yeah. I'll be down. What else do I have to do." I took the rifle from the closet and drove to town.

I turned on to Main Street from the Summers Lake road. Before I even got to the courthouse I could see sheriff's cruisers and an ambulance and a few people standing on the left side of the street at the far end of town. I parked in front of the Mark Twain Café across from the Ponderosa Motel and didn't get out of the truck right off. The door to the motel room was open and there were two ambulances in the lot. An EMT slammed the rear door of one of them and pulled out his phone and checked his messages. I saw Sarah come out of the room with Mitch and the lady from the motel. Sarah was still wearing my shirt. I waited for a semi to roll by then crossed over to the motel parking lot. The motel lady stood with Mitch watching me cross the street. She looked up at him and nodded. The two of them hustled back into the office before I got across. Sarah waited for me outside the room.

"Mitch says it looks like murder-suicide," she said. "Like they had sex, then he beat her to death and shot himself. A single pistol shot to the mouth."

"Yeah, right."

"The medical examiner did a once-over before they took her out. Found evidence of recent sexual activity," she said. We stepped inside the door. A Do Not Disturb card still hung on the knob. "But with all the blood it sure could have been rape. You have a better scenario?"

I got a whiff of the same nightclub smell of rank cologne that I first smelled up in our trailer the night we found the body had been swiped from the plane. Then there was that other smell of blood and shit and death. GQ's stupid cowboy hat was lying on the rug with blood seeping onto the brim.

"Yeah. I got a better scenario."

He was on his back sort of twisted and looking real surprised. His mouth was smashed and there was a big bruise over one eye and the top of his head was gone. I could see that from halfway across the room. And I could see how scared he'd been, like he knew that nothing he'd schemed on was ever going to work out either. Somebody had taken off his gold Rolex, the one just like his dad's. In the same fist he was holding the diabetic alert medallion I'd seen on the old man's corpse. So maybe he was finally thinking about his dad in the instant he died. Or maybe it was just butchers with a sense of humor. A Sig-Sauer lay on the carpet near his other hand and one of those little gram cocaine bottles lay half-spilled where you couldn't miss it. I could see where Nora had died too, but I didn't really want to look. I scooted out of there and waited for Sarah. She came outside about two minutes later.

"You check his DNA or bloodtype or whatever, it won't match what's on Nora. You want a match, check every damn Cuban alive or dead, especially Teófilo if you ever catch him, which I doubt."

"Teófilo?" she said.

"He's the one writing that phony narrative now."

"What?"

"Nothing."

"The owner said it was you who rented the room three nights ago," she said.

"You want to check my blood too?"

"Tommy, it's okay," she said.

"If she's beat to death, how is it okay? If everyone's dead, how is any of this okay?" I handed her the envelope with the sheets from the yellow pad.

"What's this?"

"For Mitch so he can follow along. I'll have to write him a new chapter now."

She took the envelope and stuffed it in the back pocket of her Wranglers.

"Do you want to see anything else?" She asked.

"I seen enough."

Mitch had walked out of the office and was standing by one of the ambulances talking to a guy. Sarah pinched my sleeve so I didn't head straight for my truck. The ambulance pulled out of the parking lot, going slow with no lights flashing.

"You two look bushed," Mitch said. "Come on over to the Sierra Peaks. I'll buy you a late lunch, and we can compare notes on all this. Just let me finish up here." He studied my face where I'd taken the blast of wood splinters the day before. "You oughtta get that looked at, Tom."

He headed back into the motel office.

"He can be a dick," Sarah said, "but he knows when he's being a dick." She reached up and put her hand on my neck. "I'm sure sorry," she said.

"Yeah?"

"Yeah."

"I told her to leave."

We waited for him over coffee in a booth at the Sierra Peaks. Judy looked bleary-eyed and stayed away from us, sneaking looks our way like we were on fire. Mitch came by about ten minutes later and we ordered some burgers from Al, but Al never said a word either.

"I brought in Francisco, that irrigator from Dominion's," Mitch said. "We got the Cuban kid to talk to him in Spanish. He's just seventeen, but it sounds like he's already left some bodies behind in Florida. Dang, what a crowd. He said that there's two more guys who flew into Reno all on separate flights. So now we got one in jail, one in the hospital, and maybe three on the loose."

"I guess," Sarah said.

"And all because of a fight over an estate?" he asked.

"It's a tad more complicated than that."

"No doubt about it," he said. "I like the meth angle. These guys you shot were soldiers in a drug gang. Just look at their weapons. Then take the meth lab evidence and what we found on Callie?" He looked around the room at Al and Judy. "I hate to speak ill of the dead, but that girl was dirty, I guarantee it. Word from DEA is these Mexicans are pushing meth from Argentina. Can you believe that crapola?

We can't seem to make squat in this country anymore." His radio squawked and he stopped chewing to listen.

"What about the two in the Ponderosa Motel?" Sarah asked.

"What about them?" he said. "You saw the drugs. It's like a bomb went off up here this week." He kind of grinned at me like we were friends. "The guys you killed are one thing. But this rich guy and his girlfriend. Dang. I already got emails from the Flying W aviation club, L.A. lawyers, Bloomberg Financial, and Reno Action News. We're going to have media up the ying-yang."

I had Al bring me a 7 and 7 with my burger. I wasn't on duty. I just watched Sarah get steamed.

"The dead woman was the lawyer for the dead man's stepmother," she said. "The one he was trying to scam."

Mitch just sat there for a minute. "Okay, makes sense. After yesterday no wonder he was ticked off."

"At what?" she asked.

"You two were up at Boundary Lake," he said. "You wouldn't have known."

"Known what?"

"The wife went to L.A. Superior Court again yesterday morning," he said. "The probate judge wouldn't postpone it anymore. It was on CNN last night. He declared the billionaire legally dead."

His radio squawked again.

"I gotta take this," he said. He slid out of the booth. "I guarantee you that guy's plane will never get found. There's just too much country to get lost in."

He walked to the door to the side street. We could see him talking on his radio with his free hand over his ear.

Sarah rocked to one side and pulled out the finance company envelope with the yellow sheets from her back pocket. She tore it in half and handed it to me.

Mitch wouldn't give Sarah the next day off or the day after that either. After a rough night in the chair on the tin shack porch, I left the stock out in the meadow and drove off early for Grass Valley. On the way to town I pulled into the Bonner and Tyree place and caught Dan Tyree in the screened porch of his mom's old Victorian entering calving records on his computer. We talked for a few minutes, then I drove off to see Harvey. Town was a zoo. There was a news van with a satellite dish on the roof in front of the courthouse and a couple more in the Ponderosa Motel parking lot. The lot was crammed with our own sheriffs' cars plus a couple from two different Nevada counties and a whole army of people besides. Some millionaire pal of GQ's dad was getting interviewed in front of the open motel room door as I whizzed by.

Harvey was working by the corrals when I parked under the pines at Power Line Creek. May's Honda was gone, but I waved at Harv and took off my hat and went in the cabin to look for her just in case. The place smelled like breakfast, but she wasn't around. I walked back out to the corrals.

"May took Darryl down to the dentist in Mammoth," he said.

"Tell her I stopped by."

"Are you quittin'?" He wasn't looking at me when he said it.

"Hell no. I just wanted to tell her hi, is all."

"I lost two-thirds of my help in one week," he said. "I got to take those goddamn Boy Scouts to Hornberg Lake in three days. Life don't just stop."

"I got Dan Tyree to help us."

"Damn." Harvey lit a Winston. "That'll be good. Dan looks like an old piss-head Piute hippie, but he's a hand. I thought for sure you'd come up here to quit."

"I got to go to Grass Valley today. I'll be back by tomorrow noon. Maybe even tonight."

"Better you than me. Tell 'em hi. Tell 'em—"

"Yeah. I got Lester's three-fifty-seven to give to his dad."

Harvey sort of snorted. "The cheap bastard will sell that in a week." He studied his Winston. "I'll let May know you came by. It'll mean a lot."

"I'm glad she was gone, you want to know the truth. I never know what the hell to say."

"Me neither," he said. "It's good for her to keep her mind off it."

"Hard to do with the circus in town."

"A rich prick dies, it's news," Harvey said. "The bastards didn't say a damn thing when Albert got killed, and he was a disabled vet."

"Well, I better get going. I'm going to steal some bacon and coffee for the road."

"Help yourself," he said.

"I'll bring the pack rigs up tomorrow."

"See if you got any extra lashropes."

"Okay."

By the time I got down through the sagebrush to the Reno Highway, it was past nine. I drove back through town and took an extra minute to swing by the post office and pick up our mail. It was another clear day, and warm. When I drove west toward Dominion's headquarters I looked straight into the mouth of Aspen Canyon with the Sawtooths off to the left above the sagebrush ridge and Dominion cattle on either side of the road on the new grass and the ditches overflowing with snowmelt. In twenty minutes I was past the Sonora Road in West Frémont canyon in the shade of the pines with the creek on my right and the sun on the water where Callie had died. Twenty minutes north of that and I was topping off my tank up at State Line. I didn't plan on passing any more dead people before I got to my mom's new place in Jack's Valley.

She heated up some biscuits and gravy for me, and we talked a bit. She gave me a big hug and looked at me the way she did when I was leaving for my second tour. Watching her and seeing her same old stuff in the strange kitchen made me feel almost like I was seventeen again when everything was safe and Dad was around and the most dangerous thing in the world was driving back from the hot springs in the dark with a case of beer or getting bucked off a bad horse.

Just up the road in Carson I turned on Highway 50 toward Tahoe, then circled the big lake and dropped down to I-80 at Truckee, really taking my time. I got to Lester's folks in Grass Valley a while after lunch. They had a nice house on a couple of acres out there in the oak trees and madrone. It was pretty enough country, but it wasn't my country. I stayed with them through supper and told them what I could. I let them think Lester was unconscious when the helicopter sunk. Anything else was just too awful. I gave Lester's dad the Ruger, and he told me about the big draft horse show they'd had in the fall. They wanted me to stay the night in the guest room where Lester always slept when he visited, but I said Harvey and I had an early day the next morning. I drove home four hours through the trees, down Highway 49 all the way to Placerville then back into the mountains in the dark over Echo Summit, where I could see the lights of South Shore way off through the pines, then over Luther Pass, finally winding down Monitor Pass to the Reno Highway a few miles above Dave Cathcart's under a last bit of moonrise. Then I turned south for home. I had those Indian-blanket seat covers on the Dodge with a rifle sleeve along the front edge of the bench so I could feel the stock of the Remington under my left leg. Past Piute Meadows I pulled over in Bonner and Tyree's lane and slept in the truck. I didn't figure there'd be any Cubans waiting at the pack station, but I still didn't feel like pulling in by myself after midnight and lighting the kerosene lamps and unrolling my bed in that lonesome trailer. That could wait another night or two.

I drove up at first light, corralled the stock and fixed myself breakfast. Then I haltered every horse and mule we'd taken up to North Pass and checked their feet. I tacked on one lost shoe then set to work on the sawbucks, panniers, lashropes, and tarps, laying them out on the platforms like before. When I was finished, I hoisted each set into the bed of my pickup. Harvey would fetch some of the stock later that day for the Boy Scout trip. I treated myself to a nice long session on Dave's colt before I left. It was past eleven when I finally drove down the canyon on my way to Power Line Creek.

I was just turning into town when I heard the Sikorsky. I pulled over at the Shell station and got out to look. That big Sea Stallion was thumping across the valley, flying low toward town with the Jet Ranger dangling underneath it. I knew Lester was still inside, strapped down exactly like I'd left him. Water must have just poured out of that thing when the Sea Stallion first lifted it out of the lake. It seemed half the town was standing on sidewalks or in the street, shading their eyes and looking up at those two helicopters. I saw a couple of folks holding up cell phones to take pictures. I guess it wasn't something you saw every day.

I drove through town following the choppers and parked in the sagebrush out by the reservoir. I got out to watch them land but kept my distance. Three sheriff's units, the county coroner's ambulance, a couple of Marine trucks, and civilian cars and Mike Mildenberg's wife were waiting on the airstrip, but there was no news van for him or Lester. Major Tuggle set the Jet Ranger down on the asphalt just as gentle as could be and hovered as the Marine crew pulled off the rigging. When they were done, the cables reeled back up into the Sea Stallion, and Tuggle turned the chopper to face where I was standing. He dipped the nose of the helicopter like a tip of the hat, then rose straight up, turned and whop-whopped off toward Sonora Pass. I saw Sarah standing with Mitch as an EMT opened the Jet Ranger doors. I got back in the truck and turned around, heading south before they started taking out the bodies.

Two days later we packed the Boy Scouts up to Hornberg Lake. Dan Tyree, Harvey, and I led nine mules and honchoed six saddle horses carrying the dads and Scout leaders. We herded twenty-seven Boy Scouts from Walnut Creek on foot between the horses like a mess of noisy sheep, hollering at them to stay on the trail and out of the snow. I made them form up and sound off at every piss stop and food stop and generally treated them like crap, and they loved it. We dropped them and their gear at the lake and spent the night in their camp. We headed out with the stock in the morning and would come back for them in four days so the Scouts would be in Piute Meadows in time for the Fourth of July parade.

Chapter Seventeen

Dave Cathcart was drinking iced tea with May when the three of us led the stock back down to Power Line Creek early the next afternoon. May told Harvey that a Forest Service guy had stopped by that morning and asked him to drag the dead mule off the trail at the forks of Aspen Creek before it got too rank. I told him I'd ride up as soon as we packed out the Scouts and haul back the pack saddle and bags plus his damn chainsaw.

"Can you get it done by yourself?" Dan asked.

"Probably. I may have to cut the latigos to pull the sawbuck off. Maybe I can just roll her. Depends on how ripe she is. She lit belly-down so the cinches might be pretty gross."

"Leave 'em," Harvey said.

"I'll hang 'em from a tamarack limb like scalps."

"Can you drag her uphill off the trail away from the crick?" he asked.

"Why don't you take Sarah," Dave said. "Her old gelding can haul a truck."

"I don't know if she'd want to go with me."

All four of them looked at me like I was some sort of total dipshit.

"Ask her," Dave said. "She's not doing so good."

"She saw Les's body when they took him out," May said. "I think it just broke her heart."

"She's not as tough as she thinks she is," Dave said.

"Who the hell is," Dan said.

Sarah hauled her dad's gooseneck stock trailer up to the pack station the night before the Fourth of July and unloaded her horse and saddle and a small duffle. Then I followed her to the Summers Lake campground, and we dropped off her rig so it would be waiting for us when we rode out two days later. She cooked me dinner in the trailer as we sorted our gear, and I tried to keep her cheered up with stupid Boy Scout stories. I told her how Dan Tyree really worked the Indian thing with his long hair in a braid and a magpie feather in his hatband, and how he told the little bastards that bringing their iPods and gameplayers into the high country would be disrespectful and get them all killed by the angry Piute spirits of his ancestors. The kids liked that, but Sarah's mind wasn't on the story. I told her that her lasagna was killer, but I don't think she heard. She just poured herself another glass of supermarket cabernet, which wasn't like her, and picked up Lester's chinks from the hook. She held them in front of her for a minute like she was trying on a skirt and then laid them on the table as gentle as could be, smoothing the leather flat. Then she picked up a big envelope from the Army off the bench.

"You can't," she said.

"I got to think about it. I'm twenty-six years old and I need money for college, so I might re-up for six years. It's either that or cowboy for Dominion for the rest of my life. Anyway, I haven't decided yet."

"They'd send you to Afghanistan."

"What, like it's safer here?"

When we had our food packed up and ready to go for the morning, she dragged me into the back room, stripped down to her underwear, and cried in my arms in Lester's bed until she passed out.

I slept in till six thirty. I snuck outside and pulled her big gelding out of the corral and tied him with some grain. Then I ran in the stock from the meadow and caught the other three head we'd be taking, the roan, a dun mule, and Dave's colt, and grained them too. When I went back inside, she had coffee made and was standing at the stove frying up some eggs in another one of my shirts and a pair of socks and nothing else that I could see. She looked ornery and distracted and had already burned the first batch. I got coffee and put plates and juice glasses and forks on the table. She looked out the front window.

"How many times have you ridden Dad's colt?"

"Maybe four times."

"In the corral?"

"Where else."

"It's real rocky," she said. "I wouldn't want to get bucked off there."

"I didn't plan on getting bucked off."

"You got bucked off there plenty when you were in high school," she said, cranky as hell.

"I'm not in high school. I had to really chouse him to see if he'd buck at all. He's just a big pup."

"You shouldn't ride colts by yourself."

"That's why you're here."

She kind of scowled at that.

"Mitch said a guy matching Teófilo's description chartered a jet in Reno five days ago," she said. "Paid cash to get flown down to San Francisco."

"Heading west over the mountain just like the billionaire."

"He probably caught a commercial flight back east from SFO," she said. She dumped the eggs and some sausage on the plates. "I messed them up. You don't have to eat them."

I dug in. "They aren't as bad as they look."

That wasn't the right thing to say.

"And you were right," she said. "The blood type of the semen recovered from Nora Ross didn't match GQ. We checked the Cuban kid's too. Nothing there." She fidgeted with her shirttail. "I asked them to check the two from the bridge. And the two at the snow cabin." She clanked the spatula on the skillet. "Anybody else?"

"Tony?"

That wasn't the right thing to say either.

"There was no powder residue on GQ's hands," she said. "And the round smashed two of his front teeth. I guess if you were killing yourself with a pistol to the roof of your mouth, you'd take better aim."

"You'd think."

"I just wanted to tell you you've been right about all this."

"That don't change anything."

"The Cuban kid hinted to Francisco that it was Teófilo who killed them at the motel," she said, "after he raped Nora. But the kid was too scared to come out and say it."

"Shows good sense. Even with his pals gone."

"He knows we're going to have to let him go," she said. "Even with him talking, Mitch still hasn't connected the dots. If he did his head would explode. He never even asked why you rented the motel room. He thinks you did it just to screw the pretty lawyer." She gave me a look. "The man is an idiot."

"That's why we got to lay it out for him. I got to straighten this out."

"It's like the missing plane story and the Les and Callie and Albert story came to a fork in the road," she said.

"Only in Mitch's tiny little brain."

"Every day we say nothing," she said, "makes it harder to say anything."

"Then nobody knows the truth."

She stood at the stove barelegged with her hair all over the place. When she caught me looking, she turned and walked back toward the bedroom.

I took my coffee outside with the stuff-sacks we'd laid out the night before. I loaded them with our food and kitchen junk in a pair of pack bags and set them on the platforms with my bedroll. When I came back in, she'd pulled on her Wranglers and boots, pinned up her hair, and set down to eat. The food helped her disposition.

"You think we'll be able to see the fireworks from where we camp tonight?" she asked.

"Should be. Where the plane crashed is pretty high, so we'll at least see the colors over the reservoir."

"Thanks for doing this," she said.

"Nothing like a little decomposing mule meat to re-direct the mind."

"Seriously," she said. "I need to see where it happened." She got up and took her plate to the sink.

We went outside and got to saddling. I went slow with the colt, brushing him down and laying my blankets just-so before I set Dad's saddle on his back. Sarah's horse was rigged up by the time I took the brush and swept the Horn-berg Lake trail dust from the tooling on the skirts.

"It's just going to get dusty again in twenty minutes," she said.

"That's okay." I finished brushing the saddle off, then wiped it with a rag and hobbled the colt.

I saddled the dun mule with a sawbuck but no bags. We'd pack the stuff from the dead mule on him when we got to the forks. We hoisted the loaded pack bags and the one bedroll on the roan and lashed it all down. Then I tied the mule in behind him and took the rifle scabbard over to Sarah's gelding.

"You mind carrying this? I don't want it under my leg if the colt pitches a fit."

"Sure," she said. "Are you going to lug this rifle around for the rest of your life?"

"Yes ma'am."

We strapped the scabbard under her stirrup leather. She swung up and I handed her the pack string. Then I buckled on my chinks, cheeked the colt, and stepped aboard and let Sarah lead the way up the canyon.

We didn't talk. Not for a long time. We just rode up through the sagebrush into that familiar country with the creek cutting through the meadows and the first of Bonner and Tyree's cows and calves out on the permit grass and the granite peaks up ahead, lined up one after the other with a wisp of cloud over them all. We stopped after a while up on the upper edge of the meadow on the wet grass covered with yellow monkey-flower. I rode the colt up next to Sarah and made him stand. With her watching the clouds and the ridges and finally looking sort of at peace, she reached over and put her hand on my neck and held it there for a minute the way she did. When she pulled it back, the colt must have noticed it for the first time and jumped sideways. He bogged his head and tried to buck and I could hear Sarah laugh almost like a shriek, happy and not worried at all. I let him buck a few jumps before I pulled him up and circled him back to where Sarah sat the gelding.

"Oops," she said.

"He didn't mean nothin'. He's just feeling good."

"Will I be able to see any of the plane?" she asked.

"Sure. I'll show you where we hid all the pieces. Then you'll be my partner in crime."

"I'd like that." She looked at her watch. "We're missing the parade."

"We're making our own parade."

She took off her hat and undid her hair, sort of combing it out with her fingers and half smiling to herself without looking at me as she put the hat back on.

I pushed the colt to take the lead when the trail left the meadow and wound through the old aspen where the Basques had carved their sheepherder names in the white bark a hundred years before. We stopped to let the horses drink in the next meadow, where calves stood in shallow water on the gravel of the creekcrossings and watched us until we passed. Then we rode on up the canyon a while more. We passed the two ATVs, where the Cubans I'd killed had left them in the boggy timber.

"Did they ever find that watch?"

"What do you mean?" she asked.

"Wasn't Lester wearing a watch when your crew took him out of the chopper?"

"I didn't see one," she said. "You mean the gold Rolex he took?"

"Yeah."

"He wasn't wearing a watch," she said. "And I read the coroner's report. It was real specific."

"He was wearing it when we strapped him down."

"It probably fell off," she said, "while he was struggling."

We rode on a bit. We were in the baby aspen almost to The Roughs.

"That was a good watch with a diver's clasp. It wouldn't have just come off, no matter how much he thrashed. If it wasn't on the body, that meant Lester took it off himself."

"My god, why?"

"Sinking down in that freezing dark water and scared shitless knowing he's about ten seconds from the worst kind of dying, what does he do? He reaches over and unclasps that damn watch. It was the last thing he did in this life."

She pulled her horse up. I had to circle the colt back around and ride up next to her.

"Oh, no," she said.

"Yeah. So folks wouldn't call us body robbers." I couldn't look at her. "He made me swear the whole thing was just our secret. Like we were a couple of damn kids. He was keeping his word. So he wouldn't let me down."

"Oh, Tommy."

"Goddamn that boy."

I choused the colt and rode out ahead on to The Roughs. I could hear the clank of her gelding's shoes hitting loose chunks of shale right behind me and the hollow sound of the shale sliding rock-on-rock, but I still couldn't make myself turn around.

Even taking time to drag the dead mule off the trail and pack up its gear, we would get to the patch of grass just below North Pass where we found the wreck in a couple of hours and make camp. There wouldn't be much trace of what had happened there. One more good rain and it would be as if that old boy had never hit that mountain, had never missed that pass. It would be like he was just flying around over us forever, trying to find his way home. At least that's how I like to think of it. And except for me, and now Sarah, any folks who would tell otherwise are dead. We kept on riding past The Roughs and disappeared into the trees.

Made in the USA
Monee, IL
26 January 2022

89905245R00173